"You kne
didn't y

As Spencer spoke, he brushed his lips against her ear, making Maggie tremble.

"No, I thought you were Gary." *Her fiancé, the man she was supposed to marry.*

"Liar," he whispered. Then his fingers found her chin, and he tilted her head up. She opened her mouth to tell him to stop, but he kissed her silent.

Maggie groaned at his taste, at the feel of his lips. Of course she'd known it was Spencer. He'd awakened her, like Sleeping Beauty, from five years of denying her own needs. He made her feel utterly wanton.

Spencer found her buttons and finished undoing her blouse. The feel of him on her skin made her moan. "Oh, please," she sighed. He unclasped her bra, then cupped her tenderly in his hands. She leaned in, reveling in his touch, wondering how she'd gone so long without it.

"You're where you belong, sweetheart. I know every little quirk, every secret desire."

Maggie hesitated. Her mind told her to step away. To stop this right now. She was engaged to another man. Spencer wasn't hers anymore—he never would be. *Even if he was the only man she ever truly loved....*

Dear Reader,

Tangled sheets. A slow hand moving down the center of your back. Sighs under the covers. A tender kiss that ignites the flame of passion.

Imagine yourself in a beautiful costume. For one night you're someone different. Someone daring. Music swirls, champagne flows and you know that something wicked is in the air. Imagine yourself being swept away, captive to a mysterious man in a mask who takes your breath away with a single kiss.

Sexy and fun, wicked and daring. Led to the brink of temptation... Only, this time, it isn't the wrong bed—it's the wrong closet! In the middle of a party! With the wrong man!...*or is he?*

I invite you to slip between the pages with Spencer and Maggie, to find out what once tore them apart, and what finally brings them back together. To explore how love changes everything. And how one simple mistake can lead to a whirlwind of excitement, desire and, ultimately, happiness.

So curl up in that big cozy chair, or sink into a steamy bubble bath and forget the job, the kids and the mortgage. Let *Tangled Sheets* take you away to a place filled with romance, passion and the simple truth that love conquers all.

Sincerely,

Jo Leigh

P.S. Look for my next Temptation title,
Hot and Bothered, a Blaze available in Fall 1999.

TANGLED SHEETS
Jo Leigh

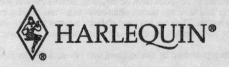

HARLEQUIN®

TORONTO • NEW YORK • LONDON
AMSTERDAM • PARIS • SYDNEY • HAMBURG
STOCKHOLM • ATHENS • TOKYO • MILAN • MADRID
PRAGUE • WARSAW • BUDAPEST • AUCKLAND

To Jan Freed, who offered such incredible
support and friendship.
Thank you, from the bottom of my heart.
And to Birgit Davis-Todd, for having such
faith and patience.

ISBN 0-373-25827-5

TANGLED SHEETS

Copyright © 1999 by Jolie Kramer.

1

MAGGIE BEAUMONT sipped her second glass of Taittinger Brut Rosé champagne as she watched Julius Caesar make a move on Tinkerbell. From the way Tink smiled and giggled, it was clear Caesar had asked her to lend him more than her ear. Maggie wished them well. At least someone was going to get lucky tonight.

Sighing and sipping, she looked around the great foyer of her mother's house, the familiar decor altered by the party planners to look like the set from *Phantom of the Opera*. They'd done a superb job. There wasn't one misstep. Food from the best caterer in Houston, the champagne chilled to the perfect temperature. Even the drapes used on the staircase had been specifically selected to contrast and flatter her gown.

This was, after all, her party, and her mother had insisted that every detail not only be perfect, but perfectly suited to her. And, since Maggie was a "winter," the color scheme didn't have one strand of "summer" or, heaven forbid, "spring." What confused Maggie now was that although everything had turned out exactly as they'd planned, she wasn't happy.

In fact, she felt annoyed, uneasy. As if there

was something big brewing on the horizon that she just couldn't see yet. On the other hand, it was quite possible that all her disquiet was directly connected to the weight of the curls piled atop her head. The extensions had been dyed to match her red hair exactly, and they did make her look vaguely like Christine, at least the one she'd seen on Broadway, but frankly it was all so heavy, she felt as if she was balancing a water jug on her head.

"You know what I love about you, Maggie?"

Maggie turned to see Fiona Drake, dressed to kill as a dragon lady, reach for a glass of bubbly. She looked sickeningly fabulous. The emerald green dress hugged her like a second skin, and the slit up her thigh was so high that each time she moved, every man in the vicinity held his breath.

"What do you love about me, Fiona?"

"That you're so calm. If this were my engagement party, I'd be running around like a madwoman, checking everyone's drinks and generally making a nuisance of myself."

"This is not calm," Maggie said. "This is standing still. There's a difference."

Fiona picked up a caviar-topped blini, then moved right next to Maggie. "Did you see that guy in the Robin Hood outfit? Someone should have warned him about the tights. I mean, come on, we all didn't need to know his religion, did we?"

Maggie laughed. "I think there's something dangerous about having a masked ball. I imagine a psychiatrist could have a field day with the costumes people choose. Sort of a Rorschach test with buttons."

Fiona turned and gave her a once-over, moving her head so she could see through her half mask. "Well, you sure picked the right dress. Virginal Christine? Perfect."

"I'm only Christine because Gary is the Phantom. There is no other significance."

"Right," Fiona said, her tone dripping with sarcasm. "I do so admire your ability to deny the obvious."

Maggie shook her head at her closest friend. Fiona was her opposite in a hundred ways, from her straight hair to her wild abandon. Everyone forgave her eccentricities because she was richer than God, and she played that for all it was worth. But the truth was, Fiona knew her better than anyone. Which wasn't necessarily a good thing. "What is it with you? Just because Gary and I are traditional—"

"Traditional? Is that what you call it? I find it positively archaic."

Maggie smiled and traded her empty champagne flute for a full one. "Not every relationship in the world is based on sex, Fiona. Gary and I have something deeper than that."

"That is such a crock. I'm telling you, you're making a huge mistake. No one in this day and age should even think of getting married before they've hit the sheets. What if you hate it? What if he likes to dress up in pink angora? Then what?"

"Gary? Pink angora?"

"It could happen."

"Fiona, you've known him as long as I have. Can you honestly tell me that you think he's got some deviant secret?"

She shook her head. "No, but then I can't believe you've been with him for two years and you haven't jumped his bones. I would have."

"I'm going to leave that one alone," Maggie said.

"And I appreciate it," Fiona said, waving to a woman decked out as Raggedy Ann.

"So where is he, anyway?" Maggie had to shout the last word as the orchestra hit the crescendo of their medley from *Cats*.

"Last time I saw him he was with Pocahontas and Marilyn Monroe."

Maggie took another sip of champagne. She should stop. She'd had more than enough. But that sense of unease lingered, made worse somehow by this little conversation with her best friend. Could it be that all she was feeling was frustration? Granted, she hadn't done the wild thing in a long time, but it hadn't bothered her in the least. Her relationship with Gary was based on other things. Respect, affection and their common backgrounds, just to name a few.

Through his law firm, he'd helped with her work at the Houston women's shelters—at least financially. He'd even agreed to make tonight's engagement party a fund-raiser. Gary wasn't quite so supportive of her other work for the shelters, but that was mostly because he thought it was dangerous. He just didn't understand how important it was to her. She felt sure that would change once they were married. He was, if nothing else, sensible.

At thirty-five, Gary was seven years older than she, and she liked that. He was a real man, not a boy. Very levelheaded, and even though he did tend to forget little things like Valentine's Day, he was still very thoughtful. He called her every day, even when he was out of town.

It was just another sign of his consideration for her and his strong traditional values that he'd asked if she'd mind waiting until the wedding night. Of course she'd agreed instantly. There was something chivalrous and proper about his request, something that suited her quest for a well-planned life. None of her decisions about Gary were based on passion. She'd been there, done that and bought the T-shirt, thank you. This time, she was using her head, not her hormones.

"Oh, God, Maggie. Get a load of Lady Godiva."

Maggie's gaze followed Fiona's pointed finger. Sure enough, Lady Godiva, hair strategically placed on all the X-rated parts, was holding court by the guest bathroom. "Who is it?"

"I think it's Tracy," Fiona said. "Yeah. Tracy."

"You're kidding. How bizarre. What was she thinking? There's practically nothing left to the imagination."

Tracy Cox had been a high school friend, and back then she'd been a shy little thing whose claim to fame had been winning the state spelling bee. Talk about a transformation. She was vamping it up for her coterie of admirers, flicking her long hair dangerously, laughing up a storm. Maggie couldn't help wondering what it would be like to be that abandoned. To care so little about her reputation. To just let go, and damn the consequences. And consequences there would be. Tracy would be a hot topic on the gossip circuit, which in River Oaks was as instantaneous and intricate as the Internet.

"It's always the quiet ones," Fiona remarked. "Do you think she's going to wear that to the reunion?"

Maggie had almost forgotten that their tenth high school reunion was coming up next week. "God, I hope so. It'll probably liven things up, don't you think?"

"Given our graduating class, it can't fail to." Fiona took another sip of champagne. "Would you look at those men? I swear, they need bibs for the drool. I'd bet the farm that every single one of them is married. With kids. And none of their poor wives understands them."

"How did you become so cynical at such a young age?"

"First, I'm not so young. Twenty-nine is rushing at me like a freight train on a greased track. And second, I'm not cynical. I'm a realist. I know what men want, and I know how to parlay that knowledge. You don't think I work out two hours a day for my health, do you?"

"Now, come on. You think all men want only one thing?"

Fiona shook her head, her long black hair swaying across her back. "No. There are some good ones. Gary, for example. But they're all taken."

"So you admit Gary does have some qualities that are worth waiting for."

Fiona turned to her. "You know I'm crazy about him, but I still think you're just crazy. Girl, you're talking about sleeping next to that man for the rest of your life. You wouldn't even buy a car without a test drive."

Maggie studied her friend's face. The bejeweled mask made her even more beautiful, highlighting her dark brown eyes and Cupid's-bow mouth. "But a car can't learn to drive better after you buy it," she said. "If things aren't perfect between Gary and me, we can work on it."

"Wrong. There's something called chemistry, kiddo. If it ain't there, it ain't there."

"I already know there's chemistry between us."

"I'm telling you, you're making a big mistake. If there was all this chemistry between you two, a court order couldn't have kept you apart this long."

"Fiona, honey. I love you. But stuff it. I know I'm doing the right thing."

"Then I'm happy for you. Honest. So go find him. I imagine he's pretty frantic by now, without you standing by his side."

Maggie sighed. "Yes, I suppose he is. Now, don't you go getting into trouble."

"The hell with that. I'm going to find Robin Hood and see just what kind of arrow he's got in that quiver of his."

Shaking her head with the knowledge that Fiona would do just that, Maggie struck out for the living room. It wasn't an easy passage. The guest list had exceeded one hundred, and adding the wait staff and the press, the place was packed. The living room had been cleared to make room for the dance floor, and although her crowd wasn't known for "shaking their booties" there were at least ten couples bravely taking a stab at the Lindy as the orchestra played Glenn Miller favorites.

Maggie nodded, smiled and gave obligatory air kisses to acquaintances, most of whom she'd met at one charity function or another. It had been her idea to have the fund-raiser, but her mother's to make it a costume ball. Maggie hadn't quibbled. There was no one in the social arena whom she trusted like her mother. Old school, Old South and old money. The combination was quite potent.

Besides, Gary and she were forever being invited here and there, and this one big extravaganza paid off many social debts. It wouldn't hurt either of them to start out their new lives together with a success like this. She only wished the noise level wasn't so high. It seemed as if everyone around her was shouting to be heard over the horn section. Although the house was large and well ventilated, the air felt thick with a hundred perfumes competing with the natural musk of human sweat. It was a veritable battlefield of sounds, scents and conversations, and the more the champagne poured, the more dangerous it became.

"Maggie! Wait!"

She turned, trying to see who'd called. A moment later, Glinda the Good Witch, complete with magic wand, came hurrying over. "Stephanie, you look wonderful."

"Thanks. So do you. That dress is fab and a half."

Maggie grinned. Stephanie was her sister's closest friend. Her father was an executive with Shell Oil, and her mother did a lot of work for City of Hope. Stephanie was in college, but she'd already declared her life's ambition was to get married, have two kids and find herself a gorgeous tennis pro.

"Have you seen Caroline? I've been searching everywhere. The only thing I can think of is that your sister took that incredible hunk she was with and pulled him into a closet."

"I haven't seen her, but I have my doubts that she'd be in a closet."

Stephanie sighed dramatically. "I know. I keep trying to get her to take a walk on the wild side, but she's so damn stodgy. I don't understand you two. You're both gorgeous, rich, smart and funny. You could have hot-and-cold-running men, but instead you both act like nuns. What a waste."

Maggie shook her head. "What is it about tonight? You're the second person to tell me I should be having sex. Is it the dress? The fact that it's my engagement party? Or maybe something's in the champagne?"

"Hmm." Stephanie tapped the star on her magic wand with a fingernail painted pastel pink to match her dress. As Stephanie shook her head, Maggie's gaze went to the diamond studs in her ears. Each oval had to be at least two carats.

"I think it's the atmosphere," Stephanie said. "I mean, it doesn't count if you're in a costume, right? Faces hidden behind masks. Pretending to be someone exotic and romantic. I swear, the air is filled with sex tonight. Can't you feel it? I've been hit on more times tonight than I can count. I've been tempted, too. Especially by that Robin Hood guy. If I thought I could be quiet enough, I'd probably go for it. But then, I'd undoubtedly get caught. I always do. I'm not like you."

"What is that supposed to mean?"

"Don't get all upset. It was a compliment. I meant that you're too much of a lady to do anything that…"

"Sordid?"

"Impetuous."

"Well, I'm quite sure Mother didn't realize her delightful little masked ball was going to turn into a sexual buffet."

"It won't. Not obviously, at least. But I wasn't kidding about the closet. Unless it was your mother's mink coat that was moaning so loudly."

"Which closet?" Maggie asked, her curiosity piqued.

"The one in the library."

"Do you really think it could be Caroline?"

Stephanie adjusted her mask, pushing it a little higher on the bridge of her small, expensive nose.

"I hope so. She could use a little insanity in her life."

"Speaking of insanity, have you seen Gary?"

Stephanie laughed. "Yeah, that is just so Gary. Why, I wouldn't be surprised if he actually drank two whole glasses of champagne!"

"Now, come on. He's not that bad."

Stephanie's smile grew kind. "No, he's not. He's a sweetie. And he's damn lucky to have you."

"Oh, stop, you're making me blush. Hey, isn't that Robin Hood over there?"

Stephanie whirled around. "See ya," she said over her shoulder.

Maggie watched Stephanie flounce toward the foyer, her big skirt brushing dangerously close to a towering platter of prawns, and wondered if Stephanie would encounter Fiona there too. But then Maggie's eye was caught by something in the corner, right by the big coat closet. Barbarella had Tarzan's hand, and she was opening the closet door. They both took quick glances to see if anyone was watching, then they ducked inside, closing the door after them.

So Stephanie was right. Sex was happening right here in her mother's house. Maggie felt her cheeks heat as she thought about the logistics involved. It couldn't be very comfortable. But it would be exciting. Dangerous. Crazy. Something she'd never do. Not with Gary, at least.

Gary was many things, but uninhibited wasn't one of them. He didn't have to be. He knew who he was, and wore his confidence like a tailored suit. His blond good looks got more than a little attention from other women, but with Gary she would never have to worry. Mostly because his work didn't allow him time for extracurricular activities. His law firm swallowed him almost whole. Almost. He always made time for her. No, Gary wasn't the kind of man who'd take her to a closet. And she wasn't the kind of woman who'd go.

There'd been a time, though, when she would have. And a man she would have done it with. *Spencer*. God, it wouldn't do to think of him tonight. Not at her engagement party. He would have had her in the closet so fast they would have made skid marks. But that was long ago. When she was still young and foolish. Luckily, she'd matured since then, and she had the life to prove it.

Except for a few little things, everything in her world was perfect. Much of that was due to Gary's influence. He was the kind of man she could look up to. Emulate. With all his business and social obligations, it was only natural that he wasn't obsessed with the baser things in life like sex. Up until tonight, and all this talk about closets and quivers, that hadn't bothered her at all. But Fiona's warning kept swirling through her mind. Was she making a mistake?

She hadn't wanted to think about it, but she was, in fact, going to be sleeping with Gary for the rest of her life. And if she was totally honest with herself, that idea wasn't a hundred percent appealing. It wasn't that she didn't find him handsome. In fact, he was a little too good-looking. Tall, broad shoulders, slim waist. And she liked his kisses well enough. So what was it? Probably the only reason she wasn't excited about her future sex life with Gary was that she hadn't let herself get excited. It only made sense that since she knew they weren't going to do anything until the wedding night, she hadn't let her imagination run wild. But what if that wasn't it? What if they really didn't click? Oh, God. Maybe she *had* made a mistake. Maybe Fiona was right. She grabbed another glass of champagne from a passing waiter. As she sipped, the idea consumed her. What if sex with Gary was awful?

Wait. She was getting crazy for nothing. If being with Gary didn't make the bells ring and the whistles blow, then so what? They could still have a very satisfying life. The emphasis would simply be on other things. She'd had one marriage that was based on passion. That marriage, despite bells and whistles of epic proportions, had ended in dismal failure. Surely this relationship was much more sensible. It wouldn't hurt, however, to have a *little* passion, would it? After all, Gary had all the qualities she wanted in a husband. Well, almost. No, that wasn't fair. She had no right to say that when she hadn't even given him a chance.

She looked again at the big coat closet. No. She couldn't. He wouldn't. It was crazy even entertaining such a thought.

"Congratulations, Maggie."

She jumped, sure for a moment that she'd been

caught with her libido showing, but then she calmed herself, certain that no one could possibly know what she'd been thinking.

"I know you and Gary are going to be so happy together."

Maggie smiled at Alice Porter, the woman who ran the law clinic that handled most of the *pro bono* work for the women's shelters. She was dressed as one of the Andrews Sisters, and the uniform worked. She'd never seen Alice, who was close to her mother's age, in anything but rather boxy suits. She was actually quite lovely like this. "Thanks, Alice."

"I was just telling your father that I've never met a more sensible couple than you two. How many young people would be socially conscious enough to make their engagement party into a fund-raiser?"

"Socially conscious. Yep, that's us. Always ready to do our part for the greater good."

Alice tilted her head slightly, giving Maggie a bewildered look.

She shouldn't have made that comment, not to someone she didn't know well. But then, there were only three or four people at this party she did know well enough to talk plainly to. "I'm just delighted that we can help, even in this small way," she said, smiling as brightly as she could. "Did I mention how wonderful you look?"

Alice's expression changed immediately to one of pleasure. When in doubt, use a compliment. It worked for her mother, and it worked for Maggie.

"Please excuse me," she said, thinking that a

quick departure wouldn't be amiss. "And don't forget to try the pâté." She left Alice, and headed toward the dining room. As she passed the big closet she heard it. A female voice. A moan. Filled with illicit desire and wicked abandon.

Right then and there Maggie made up her mind. Tonight was her night. Gary was going to be her husband in less than a month. She was going to find out if there were bells and whistles, by God, and she was going to find out right now.

As she hurried on, she became more and more aware of what Stephanie had alluded to. The air *was* filled with sex tonight. People were touching each other, and not just on the arm. Right in front of her, two couples stood side by side. Cleopatra and John Wayne were so close it looked as if they were conjoined twins. Rambo had his hand on Olive Oyl's back. Her lower back. And still descending. This, despite the fact that Olive had been married to Popeye for seven years.

Maggie passed them just as Rambo's hand hit pay dirt. She heard Olive's giggle over the soft strains of "Send in the Clowns." Finally, she caught sight of Caroline. It was hard to miss her sister with that feather sticking straight up out of her headband. She made a very pretty Pocahontas. Maggie waved, and then she saw Gary.

He stood next to Caroline, looking odd and sinister in his Phantom getup. The costume was so detailed she'd barely recognized him when she'd seen him in it for the first time. Only a small portion of his face was uncovered by the mask, and even that was disguised with makeup. He'd even agreed to wear the black wig under his fedora after a lot of cajoling on her part.

But she could see his blue eyes—well, one of them at least. Actually, the makeup made the eye seem darker somehow. Wider, too. Even his smile seemed unfamiliar with all that lipstick and with only the left half visible.

Her stomach tightened as she thought about what she was about to do. There was every possibility that Gary would object. That he'd be shocked by her behavior. If they were caught, it would cause a scandal. Tarnish his reputation, and her own. On the other hand, this might be exactly what they both needed. The one thing that would make their relationship complete.

The closer she got, the more nervous she became. Her breathing grew rapid, and she could feel her heart thumping in her chest. The important thing was to just do it. No second guesses this time. Just action.

"Hey, Maggie, guess who—"

Maggie ignored her sister. She went straight to Gary, took him by the hand and then pulled him after her.

"Hey," Caroline cried. "What? Wait! Maggie!"

Nothing was going to stop her. Not the congratulations coming from their guests, not the tightness in her chest, not even the little warning voice that told her to stop, now, before it was too late.

She just kept on walking, pulling Gary behind her, straight past the foyer and the living room, all the way to the library. The closet door was open, and she let out a pent-up breath. This was it. The moment that was going to determine the course of her married life.

She walked to the closet, pushed Gary inside, stepped over the threshold and closed the door behind her.

2

IT WAS DARK. Very dark. But that wasn't a bad thing. In fact, it was a bonus she hadn't planned on. Before she could lose her nerve, she ran her hand up Gary's chest until she found his face. A second later, his mask was on the floor and so was hers. She took one last deep breath and leaned in to give him the kiss she'd held back for two years.

He made a noise that she took to mean he was pleased, although it might just indicate surprise. No matter. As long as he didn't stop her, she was going to go through with this. Leaning in even closer, she deepened the kiss, teasing his lips open, and then his teeth. He tasted like champagne.

Then, just as she moved her right hand down his chest, Gary kissed her back. Now it was her turn to be surprised. Something...happened. Something good. Oh my. She'd had no idea he could kiss like this. Why in the world hadn't he done this before? So they'd both been holding out! God, maybe he had a thing for closets. She didn't care. If he'd kiss her like this, she'd *live* in a closet.

Moaning her pleasure, she felt an almost forgotten sense of pure wicked abandon. She continued her exploration, inching her fingers past his waist, down his pants.

It wasn't difficult to tell that he was enthused about this impromptu liaison. And growing more enthused by the moment. Holy cow, had she been crazy?

"I can't believe we've waited so long to do this," she whispered. "That you never..."

His hand around her waist chased her words away. He pulled her tightly against him so she could feel him from shoulder to thigh. His body seemed harder somehow, broader. Funny what a kiss could do. He moved, and she objected, but only for a second. How could she complain, when he'd discovered the crook of her neck? She certainly had no objections to him using his tongue in such devious ways. She practically swooned in his arms as he dipped his head to her cleavage.

She heard something then, right outside the door. She froze. He started to say something, but she quickly put her fingers to his lips. "Shh," she whispered.

He kissed her again, and all thoughts of the world outside the closet disappeared. The next thing she knew, he'd turned them both around until she was supported by the coats. He pressed against her, yet she wanted him closer. Feeling foolish and giddy, she took his hand in hers and brought it down to knee level. Then she started lifting her skirt, showing him what she wanted.

"Ma—"

Again, she put her fingers to his lips. "Shh," she said, guiding his hand once more.

He took over, bunching the material until she felt the skirt and petticoat skim over her legs and thighs, and he didn't stop until the costume was scrunched around her middle. She cried out in delicious surprise when she felt his hands boldly explore her hips, her thighs, and then between her thighs.

"Oh, wow," she whispered. "Oh, dear." Then she quieted again, the awareness that someone could open the door any second making her tremble with excitement.

He kissed her deeply as his hands stayed busy. Hooking his thumbs under the band of her panties, he lowered them slowly, slowly down her legs.

Her heart pounded in her chest and in her temples. She hadn't really believed it would be like this. She hadn't even been sure she wanted to go all the way with him. But now, with his mouth on hers, it would take the end of the world to stop her. She felt so brazen, so wanton. So Fiona.

It had been too long since she'd felt like this. Five years. How could she have been so wrong? She'd thought, all this time, that only one man could make her feel this way. That only one man could steal her breath, make her knees grow weak and create such a fire inside her.

Fool! She'd been such a dope. Gary had magic hands, kissed like the man in her dreams. He knew instinctively what she wanted, and teased her with the knowledge.

The dress was in her way as she reached out for him. Instead, she had to reach back and hang on to her mother's fur coat. She wished there was a light in here so she could see his face. But then she felt his hot breath on her stomach, and she closed her eyes, not missing the light at all.

From then on, all she could do was hang on for dear life. It couldn't just be that she hadn't had sex in so long. It couldn't be that her body was so ready that she climaxed just from the way he teased her with his mouth, and again when he stood up and made love to her until she had to muffle her screams on his neck. More was at work here. Gary somehow knew exactly what she liked, and what she craved.

As she struggled to regain her breath, all she could think of was that for two years she'd been with a wolf in sheep's clothing. How was it possible? She'd really believed she knew Gary. He'd never exhibited this part of his character, not once.

His kisses in the past had been nice. Warm, sweet, but proper. Nothing like this burning, urgent fire. His touch had been tender, tentative. But now he ran his hands over her body as if he wanted to possess her very flesh.

He stood flush against her once more, and she tasted the sin on his lips. Dropping her skirt, she wrapped her hands around his neck and teased him with her tongue until she heard his moan.

Then, and only then, did she stop. Pull slowly away. Breathe again. Feel the lumpy cushion of coats against her back. After several moments and a few calming breaths, she felt a little more normal. More quickly than she could have imag-

ined, she became aware of her surroundings.
Aware that they were, in fact, in a closet. Maggie
tried to pull herself together, although she knew
her hair would need a mirror. Gary bumped her
in the ribs twice in his hurry to do the same. Once
she figured she'd given him enough time to be decent, she opened the door.

The coast was clear. But she didn't leave yet.
She closed the door once more, and kissed him
lightly on the lips, jumping a little when her
cheek touched his cold mask. "I never dreamed
we could ever be like this together," she whispered. "I'm so glad, because it's something I like
to do. A lot."

He stopped her with his fingers on her lips. She
understood. Words weren't adequate, and then of
course, there was the danger.

This time, she didn't even glance back. She
opened the door and dashed across the room,
down the hall, and into the rest room. Once again,
she'd made it without being caught. Locking the
door behind her, she faced herself in the mirror to
begin repairing the damage, and more impor-
tantly, to try to understand what had just happened.

Good Lord, she looked like a woman who'd
just had sex in a closet! Although *her* lipstick was
gone, most of Gary's was on her neck. Big smears
of white, black and red streaked her cheeks, and
even her breasts. Thank goodness no one had
seen her mad dash to safety. Her hair, with its
mass of curled and teased extensions, was positively electrified. As if she'd been struck by light-

ning. The image made her smile. She wasn't that far off. Seeing Gary in this new light was like a bolt from the blue. As she got the hairbrush from underneath the sink, she tried to figure out why. What signs she'd missed. Certainly a nature as passionate as his couldn't have sprung fully formed at the moment. He'd have to have been born this way. So why did he live his life as if this wasn't a part of him?

Grabbing a washcloth, she wiped away the stains that marked her. By the time she was finished, there wasn't a trace of the Phantom on her. Then she began the daunting task of taming her hair, and that took her concentration for several minutes. But then a thought stilled her hand. Perhaps Gary was afraid. Afraid of the wildness that lived inside him. Afraid that once he let it out, he wouldn't be able to pretend to be the old Gary again.

Truth be told, it scared her, too. What he'd done to her couldn't be controlled. That kind of intensity made logic disappear, decorum fly out the window. It made a person do foolish things. Hurtful things.

The whole reason she'd decided to marry Gary was that, with him, she knew her head would lead, and her heart—her lust—would never again take her to the brink. The last time had almost killed her.

Of all the complications that could have come from her moment of daring, this was the last one she'd ever considered. Now she realized she'd been completely prepared for a mediocre response to his touch. That making love with Gary would be pleasant, that's all. She'd welcomed the fact that he wouldn't stir her blood. The rest of her life would then proceed at its rightful pace. Her work, her marriage, her standing in the community—they would all come first. Now he'd turned everything upside down.

Maybe it was a fluke. A trick of the night, of champagne. Gary never drank. This could all be a result of too much bubbly and not enough food. If that were the case, then she was safe. At least for the most part. It wouldn't hurt to buy some Taittinger once or twice a year. But, for the most part, she'd want him sober and sane. The Gary she'd come to like, even admire.

She put down the brush. Her lipstick was history, but that couldn't be helped. At least she didn't look as if she'd just gotten out of bed. Although tonight, who would have noticed?

Checking her image one last time, she saw that her bodice was unbuttoned, showing quite a bit of her décolletage. A shiver went through her as she remembered his hands, and his lips, dipping into her cleavage. *What the hell*, she thought. *When in Rome.*

She left the bathroom without buttoning up, and nearly bumped into a rather tipsy Cinderella who clearly had an urgent need to get into the bathroom. Oddly enough, that calmed her down a bit.

It was safe now to find Gary. At least safe in terms of decorum. But for the first time since she'd met him, she felt a knot of nervous tension in her stomach. Gary—sweet, calm, predictable Gary. What had she done? One moment of abandon. One slip. One error in judgment! All she'd wanted were bells and whistles. Not a sixty-four-piece orchestra.

"Where have you been?"

She turned at Fiona's voice. "In the bathroom," Maggie said, hoping Fiona wouldn't see the blush she felt.

"You forgot something."

Maggie immediately patted her skirt. Could she have left her petticoat in the closet? Or worse, her panties? "Oh no," she said. "Does it show? Can you tell?"

"Now, that's interesting," Fiona said. "I was referring to your mask. Can I tell what?"

Maggie knew there was no hiding her blush now.

"So, what were you doing in the bathroom?" Fiona asked. "And with whom?"

"Nothing. I was just brushing my hair, that's all."

"Uh-huh."

"Stop it, Fiona. I wasn't doing anything. I have to go see to the guests." Maggie started to leave, but Fiona caught her arm.

"No you don't. You're not leaving until you tell me."

"Please let me go."

"Like hell. Come on, Maggie. Spill."

Maggie sighed and turned back to face Fiona. Knowing her friend, there was no way she was going to get out of this with a fib. Fiona was uncanny in her ability to sniff out a lie. "I was with Gary, that's all," she confessed, lowering her voice to make sure only Fiona could hear.

"With? How with?"

"*With* with."

Fiona's eyes widened behind her mask. "No kidding?"

Maggie nodded.

"Oh my God! Here? In front of all these people?"

Maggie crossed her arms. "We didn't sell tickets, Fiona."

"Where? How? Did you do it in the bathroom? In the shower?"

"No."

"In the backyard?"

"No. We did it in the closet."

Fiona screeched. Loudly. Every person in the area turned to stare. Maggie thought seriously about sending Cinderella to the pumpkin patch and locking herself in the bathroom for the duration of the night.

"So, come on! Tell me. Was he good?"

"Fiona, would you please keep it down?" Maggie smiled and nodded at Lancelot. "I don't need this in tomorrow's paper, okay?"

"Okay," Fiona said, lowering her voice to a conspiratorial whisper. "But tell me. I'm dying here."

"Oh, all right. He was good."

"How good?"

Maggie suddenly found she couldn't look her friend in the eye. "Very good."

"Oh?"

"Very, very good."

"Oh my God."

"Would you stop saying that?"

"I'm just so...so proud of you."

"Proud?"

"You did it. At a party. In your mother's closet, for heaven's sake. This is big. This is enormous."

"It is not. We're going to be married in a matter of weeks. You're the one who was so damn anxious for me to take a test drive."

"But I didn't know you were going to take it at the Indy 500!"

"If you don't lower your voice, I'm going to strangle you with your own hair."

"Okay, okay." Fiona's smile looked painful. "Wow, I just didn't think you had it in you, honey. Good for you."

"Thanks. I think. Now, if you're finished, I need to go find Gary. We still have guests." She started walking toward the living room, and Fiona joined her.

"So, did you instigate this little closet rendezvous?"

"I don't want to talk about it."

"Sure you do."

"No, I don't."

"I tell you everything."

"That's because you're a closet exhibitionist."

"No, honey. Tonight *you're* the closet exhibitionist."

Maggie giggled. Then she made the mistake of looking at Fiona. She burst out laughing, and that was it. Maggie couldn't walk. Or talk. All she could do was hold her stomach and laugh. Tears came to her eyes and her side ached, and everyone stared at the two of them, but she couldn't stop. She tried. But every time she looked at Fiona, she cracked up again.

"What's going on, you two?"

Maggie turned, and there was Gary, his costume so perfect, no one would ever suspect a thing. How he'd managed to get his makeup back on so perfectly after leaving so much of it on her body was a mystery, but Gary had always been resourceful. She fought another urge to burst out laughing, then took a deep breath. Finally, she felt in control once more.

"Hey there, big guy," Fiona said, her voice still too filled with humor. "We were just talking about—"

"The party," Maggie said, turning to give Fiona the evil eye. "How much fun everyone seems to be having."

"I'll say," Fiona muttered under her breath.

Maggie was just close enough to give her a shot with her elbow.

"Ow."

"Hmm?" Gary said, looking from Maggie to Fiona and back again. "What?"

"Nothing." Maggie took Gary's hand, and started to lead him toward the shrimp table. Food was always a good distraction.

"I was just having a conversation with Dwayne Anderson," Gary said, his voice the essence of calm. "You remember him from the philharmonic society? I think they're looking for new counsel, and honestly, I think he was checking me out. I'd like to take him to dinner next week. Maybe to Café Annie.''

Maggie was amazed at how steady his voice sounded. How he was able to act as if nothing at all had happened. Was it possible the closet hadn't been a big deal to him? That it was just a walk in the park? No. What had occurred was a very big deal. But this wasn't the time or place to go on about it. If he could control himself, then so could she. As long as she didn't look at Fiona. ''I think that's a great idea. We've got next Thursday open. No, wait. Not next week. Friday is the reunion, and I'll be too crazy. I'll pencil it in for the week after.''

''Good, good. Oh, and I mentioned to your father that I thought we ought to become members of the Houstonian. He said he'd take care of it for us. I think that's great, don't you?''

''Absolutely,'' she said, glad once again that Gary and she were so in sync. The Houstonian health and fitness club was exactly the kind of place they should be seen. Exclusive, expensive and filled with people who would be very useful to Gary in his career.

They rounded the corner, and Maggie saw Caroline's feather bobbing above the crowd at the buffet tables. She steered Gary in that direction, aware that Fiona was still tagging along, as indicated by the sound of a muffled giggle.

When they neared her sister, Maggie saw her parents. As Marie Antoinette and Louis XVI, they were hard to miss. She let go of Gary's hand and reached up to adjust a wayward curl. Just as she realized it was a hopeless task, she heard Fiona gasp.

Maggie turned, and gasped herself. Standing right next to her sister was a second Phantom. His costume was a duplicate of Gary's. From the mask, to the cape, right down to the shoes. Identical. Except for the smeared makeup.

The crowd parted before her. Flashbulbs exploded in a burst of lights. The second Phantom reached for his mask, and slowly removed it. Then he smiled. "Hi, Maggie."

"No," she said, feeling the blood drain from her face.

"Yes," he said, with a smile she just now recognized.

"It's not possible," she said, looking first at Caroline, then her parents, desperate for an explanation. Her mother seemed as taken aback as she herself felt. But her father and Caroline looked remarkably nonplussed, almost smug. They had some serious explaining to do.

"Oh, but it is possible," the impostor said, moving closer to her. Now that she knew it was him, all the signs glared at her. The breadth of his shoulders. The dangerous arch of his eyebrow. The self-possession that had bewildered her from the first. She stepped back, afraid of his touch.

"What in hell are you doing here?"

"I came to congratulate you on your upcoming wedding."

"But…"

"And I have to say, I've never been welcomed so delightfully in my life."

"I'm sorry," Gary said, pushing his way forward. "Have we met?"

"No, we haven't had the pleasure. I'm Spencer Daniels. Maggie's ex-husband."

3

SPENCER COULD HARDLY believe how well things were going. Much better than he'd anticipated. Perfectly, in fact. He'd never dreamed she would be the one to start the ball rolling, so to speak. He hadn't felt this exhilarated in years. He supposed he should feel guilty because she'd thought he was her intended, but he didn't. True, a gentleman would have pointed out her error. But he wasn't a gentleman. Not when it came to Maggie. That's why she'd married him, although he doubted she'd ever admit it.

"Well, well," Gary said, holding out his hand. "Nice to meet you, Spencer. Maggie's told me so much about you."

Spencer took Gary's hand, not surprised somehow that it was a little damp and that he squeezed a little too hard. "I hope you won't hold that against me."

Gary chuckled, but it wasn't very convincing. "Great costume," he said. "How'd you think of it?"

Spencer looked at Caroline, who stepped behind her father. "I guess I misunderstood the invitation," he said. "I didn't realize the groom-to-be was supposed to be the only Phantom."

"No harm done," Gary said. "The more the merrier."

Maggie coughed sharply, and Fiona, who looked rather spectacular herself, turned around and grabbed a glass of champagne from a passing waiter. From the look of it, Maggie had shared their little secret with Fiona. Not too surprising, since they'd shared every secret since grade school. At least Fiona didn't look as though she wanted to kill him.

He went over to his old friend and kissed her on the cheek. "Hi, beautiful."

"Welcome back," Fiona said, trying hard to hide a wicked grin and failing miserably. "That was one hell of an entrance."

"I do my best," he said, smiling as he turned his attention back to Maggie, who looked as if she not only wanted to kill him, but kill him slowly, with rusted instruments. But it also looked as if she might pass out before she had the chance. He smiled. He'd wanted her off balance. Maybe not 911 off balance, but he had the feeling she'd recover soon. Maggie's breeding didn't allow for public displays of emotion. Just to be on the safe side though, he took another step toward her.

She scurried back, holding out her hand like a shield. "Don't come any closer," she said.

"But..."

"I'm warning you. You stay right where you are. Or better yet, leave. Just leave."

He had no intention of leaving. It was far too early in the game.

"Margaret!" her mother said. "Please, not so

loud. Does everyone here have to know our business?"

Spencer watched as Maggie pulled herself together. Her shoulders went back, her chin lifted. But the panic still made her eyes wide. Wide and beautiful. Even more beautiful than in his dreams. He swallowed, unprepared for the way his gut tightened. He hadn't counted on that.

She turned calmly to Louis XVI. "Daddy, make him leave."

Her father looked at her for a moment, then at his wife, then at Spencer. Frank's gaze lingered for a long, uncomfortable moment, then he turned once more to his daughter. "He's always been welcome in this house. I see no reason to change that now."

Maggie's mouth dropped open, but her reaction was nothing compared to Betty's. Her fan stopped, her towering head of white hair quivered and her powdered cheeks reddened. "Frank!" she said.

The man in question looked at his wife with a determination his makeup couldn't hide. He wasn't going to budge, despite the fact that it was very evident he was going to pay, and pay dearly, for his traitorous stance.

Spencer tried not to let his pleasure show. He'd always admired Frank Beaumont. The man was quiet, but he had backbone. He'd been good to Spencer, even after the divorce. Nicer than his own father by a long shot.

But he'd have to thank Frank later. Right now he had to defuse the situation at hand. A casual glance told him many ears were tuned in to the little group. He couldn't afford to have things crescendo too soon. His comeback had several steps, and this was just the first. He smiled brightly at Maggie. "I'm surprised, princess," he said, shaking his head, "and wounded. I thought we were friends."

"Don't you princess me, you...you...*snake*."

"Me? Maggie, love, all I wish for you is happiness. Marital bliss. I'm here to see you get everything you deserve. Nothing less."

Maggie's eyes narrowed with suspicion. "What's that supposed to mean?"

He crooked a painted eyebrow. "Just that I came to offer you my heartfelt best wishes for your future happiness."

She flushed, and he knew she wasn't buying it. It didn't bother him. He liked that she didn't know what to expect. But she wasn't the only one off-kilter. God, but she still had the power to take his breath. Her hair, a red so dark on first glance it looked black. He'd memorized the million shades of scarlet that shimmered in the light. Of course, when he'd known her, she hadn't had so much of it, but it still looked damn good.

His gaze moved to her skin, so soft and elegant he'd been afraid to touch her that first night. So supple and yielding he'd had to force himself not to touch her twenty-four hours a day. And who could forget her eyes. What he'd learned about Maggie from her eyes! She was an open book, if one knew how to read her. And he did. It wasn't that they were such a dark blue, or that they were so perfectly almond shaped. Maggie's eyes simply telegraphed her every emotion. From fear, to delight, to passion. Passion. Despite everything, despite her calling him a snake, he could see the telltale signs right there in her gaze.

No, making his entrance had gone perfectly. It was everything he'd hoped for and much more. He'd never dreamed she would be in his arms so quickly. So willingly. Of course she'd say she hadn't known it was him. But that first kiss had been a dead giveaway. It had almost knocked him to his knees. Hell, it had almost made him reconsider his plan. Almost.

Maggie turned away to pluck the half-empty champagne glass from Fiona, which she polished off in one gulp.

Spencer decided his best bet was to work on Betty. Frank had declared himself, and now, after he'd seen Gary's costume, he realized just how much Caroline was in his corner. Maggie's little sister hadn't mentioned he'd be in the same costume as the groom. She'd just sent him the box, which included the mask, the cape, the hat and the makeup, complete with instructions on how to put it all on.

He turned to Betty, the one person who could blow the whole deal, and smiled. "You look wonderful," he said. "And this party is another feather in your formidable cap."

She flushed and fluttered her fan. "Save the flattery, young man. Despite what my husband says, I don't appreciate you barging into our home. This is Maggie's night. I won't have it spoiled."

"I don't intend to spoil it. You have my word, Betty, I'm not here to ruin this wonderful party. I truly want what's best for Maggie, that's all."

She eyed him for a long while, which was disconcerting given that one of her false eyelashes was on crooked. But he kept the eye contact steady. He knew Betty wasn't going to be a friend, but he didn't want her as an active foe. She had too much influence over Maggie.

"Well," she said, shaking her head.

He gave her one of his most charming smiles, but he couldn't be sure of its effect, given the stupid makeup.

She didn't welcome him with open arms, but on the other hand, she didn't call the police. He decided to strike once more while the iron was hot. Purposely ignoring Maggie, he turned to Frank. "You have room for an ex-son-in-law for a few days? Until next Saturday?"

Before Betty or Maggie had a chance to respond, Frank nodded. "Of course there's room. You can stay in the guest house."

"What!"

Spencer had to hide his delight at Betty and Maggie's simultaneous protest. Betty would now be focused on her errant husband, which left him to concentrate on Maggie. The closer he looked at her shocked expression, the more it told him. If she hadn't felt what he had in the closet, she wouldn't have given a damn if he stayed here or not. *The lady doth protest too much*, he thought.

There was only one conclusion he could come to. Maggie Beaumont still had a thing for him. Which was the damn cherry on top.

"He is not staying here," she said. "And he's certainly not staying in the guest house."

"Margaret, it's just for a week," Frank said. "Isn't that right, Spencer?"

He nodded. "Just until after the reunion. I'll have found a house by then."

"A house?" Maggie's eyes got very large. "You're not moving here, are you?"

"That I am, princess. I'm coming home."

She shook her head, her wild curls making the move very dramatic. "I don't believe this," she said, moving closer to him. She poked him in the chest with her finger. "I'm marrying Gary." She poked him again. "I'm very happy."

He grabbed her hand, wanting to tell her that she could have been happy with him, if only she'd believed in him. He wanted to show her his stock portfolio, show her the net worth of the businesses his venture capital had funded. But he didn't. He simply let her go.

"I'm not going to let you ruin this," she said.

Her lips might say no but, dammit, her eyes said something else. What he saw there was turmoil laced with fire. He knew that because he'd seen it before. He'd seen it just before they'd gotten married. After they'd moved in together. Every time they'd made love. If the light had been on in that closet, he would have seen it there too. The look clinched the deal for him. If he'd had any doubts before, they were erased by the look in her eyes.

She must have seen something equally telling in his eyes, because she ripped her gaze away, turning to her fiancé. "Gary, say something," she said, yanking her hand out of Spencer's grip. "Tell him to leave."

Gary coughed. He walked over to Maggie and wrapped his hand around her waist, like he was the King of Siam and she was Anna. He pulled her against him, then smiled, an elegant, practiced grin meant to placate but not give in. Or was that only his makeup?

"I've got a spare room at my place," Gary offered. "It's not much, but you're welcome."

Spencer had to think a minute. He'd assumed, especially after that handshake, that Gary wasn't going to be an issue. But the guy had some backbone after all. With all he'd learned about the man, he hadn't been able to predict this. But he should have known Maggie wouldn't pick a loser. "Thanks, old man," he said, "but I want to catch up with Frank and Betty. It's been a long time since I've been home, and I don't want to miss the opportunity."

Gary pulled Maggie back a little farther, not exactly behind him, but in that general direction. He seemed to stand a little taller, too. "I can understand that," he said, his voice low and, if possible, even smoother. "But it appears Maggie isn't happy with the arrangement."

So it was going to be like this, eh? Spencer squared his own shoulders and prepared to do battle. He wouldn't use force—that was something he hadn't succumbed to since high school. But he'd have his way, nonetheless. He hadn't made it this far just to let this lawyer get the better of him.

Gary's hand dropped from Maggie's waist. The noise around them seemed to diminish. Maggie pushed herself between the two men, her gaze darting frantically from one to the other. "Stop it, right now. Both of you. People are listening."

Then a flashing light popped right in front of Spencer's face, followed by two more flashes in quick succession. He held up his hand, trying to blink away the spots in his eyes.

"Hey!"

He heard Maggie's voice, but he still couldn't see.

"What are you doing?" she asked the photographer.

"Getting a scoop for the front page," he said.

"No you don't," Maggie said. "You give me that film right now."

"Are you kidding? Give up two Phantoms? Fighting over Christine? Come on, lady. It's the first vaguely interesting thing that's happened all night."

"Do you know who my father is?" Maggie said imperiously.

Spencer recognized the tone all too well. And the words. His vision cleared just in time to see the photographer make a beeline for the door. Maggie turned to Spencer, pushing him forward. "Do something."

He didn't go. Not yet. He wasn't sure if he wanted the paper to run the picture or not. Before he could decide, Caroline darted past them. "I'll go," she said. "You guys figure out what to do with Spencer."

Then she was gone. The whole room had stilled, and everyone stared at the little group in the middle. Fiona shook her head. "If he wants a photo scoop, he should try a few of the coat closets."

Maggie gasped, then walked over to her best friend. "Fiona, I know you're outspoken, but what I can't figure out is by whom."

Fiona blinked and Spencer grinned. This was more like it. This was the girl he remembered. Maggie the Magnificent. Able to cut down egos in a single bound. Pulling out bons mots at the drop of a catty remark. He'd been afraid the years had cowed her. They hadn't. Not entirely at least. He'd thought about that often. What kind of a woman Maggie would turn out to be. So far, he liked what he saw. Except for her association with the barrister, of course.

It was clear Fiona had realized her faux pas. She bit her upper lip, gave Maggie a weak grin, then started walking backward in tiny steps. "Where is that waiter?" she said, the guilt lacing each word. "I'm so thirsty I could…"

She didn't finish the sentence. Leaving the door wide open for Gary's question. "What did she mean?"

Maggie turned to face her Phantom. "Oh, you

know Fiona. Always sticking her size-six feet in her size-twelve mouth."

"But what was she talking about? What's in the closet?"

Maggie put her hand on Gary's chest. "Nothing, honestly. You know Fiona," she repeated.

The interplay was fascinating. Spencer didn't think Gary believed her, but Maggie was batting her eyelashes. The guy didn't stand a chance.

"Well, we still haven't solved the basic issue here," Gary said, sounding like the lawyer he was. He turned to Spencer, his frown losing some of its punch because of the lipstick. "I have to say, Spencer, I'm not thrilled with the idea of you staying in the guest house."

"It's only for a few days," Spencer said, making sure his voice didn't sound the least combative. "You don't have a thing to worry about. You two are rock solid, right? Two hearts about to be one? Lovers, soul mates, friends?"

Gary didn't stop frowning. "Yes, but—"

"Good, then it's settled." Spencer turned to Betty and Frank. "I appreciate your hospitality."

Betty sniffed disdainfully, but Frank nodded. He put his hand on his wife's shoulder, and Spencer knew the debate was over.

Then he turned to face Maggie who looked at him with the kind of furious glare usually reserved for mass murderers. "I'll let you get back to your guests," he said. "I'm going to go make sure no one else mistakes me for the groom."

MAGGIE WATCHED Spencer walk toward the shrimp and pondered taking the heavy ice sculpture and knocking him over the head with it. But then she'd have to spend the night in jail, and just the thought of the sheets was enough to keep her on the straight and narrow.

It had started out to be such a nice party. Pretty costumes. Great food. Enough champagne to seed a whole new chapter of AA. Spencer had ruined it all.

She still couldn't quite believe what he'd done to her. Pretending to be Gary so she'd drag him into the closet. The nerve. The brass. He hadn't changed. Not one iota in all these years. He'd always been able to turn her world upside down. At least he was consistent.

She couldn't bear to think about what they'd... how she'd...where he'd... She buried her face in her hands and whimpered.

"Maggie?"

She opened her fingers and looked at Gary. If he ever found out, ever suspected, he'd hate her forever. She wouldn't blame him. Her blunder seemed ludicrous even to her. How could she have ever mistaken Spencer for Gary? Even in the costume. Even in the dark. Even after all that champagne. It was inexcusable. She was a rat. A traitor. An idiot.

"I'll go fetch him back," Gary said. "I won't have him upsetting you like this."

She reached out and grabbed the back of his cape. "No, no, wait."

He stopped.

"It's only for a few days. It's fine. I'll be too

busy to even notice him Honestly, let's just let it go."

"Are you sure?"

She nodded. "Mother and Dad will take care of Spencer," she said, then turned to her parents. "Won't you?"

"Yes, we will," Betty said. "You can be assured that Spencer won't be interfering in any way. I guarantee it." She touched Gary gently on the shoulder. "Now you two go off and do some dancing. This is your special night! Enjoy it. I have to go find out why I haven't seen one miniature quiche walk by in the last hour."

Maggie would have been surprised to see a miniature quiche walk by any time, but she thought it best to keep that to herself. Her father strolled after her mother, and she couldn't help imagining what was in store for him after the guests had gone. He rarely crossed her mother, and never so publicly. What Maggie couldn't understand was why he'd done it tonight. He knew what Spencer had done to her. So why hadn't he kicked his ex-son-in-law out the door and up the street? It didn't make sense.

She tried to think logically, but the orchestra suddenly seemed far too loud, the crowd too oppressive, and the air too thick. She needed to get out of here. She headed toward the foyer where things were a little quieter.

"I'm not happy about this," Gary said.

Damn, she'd almost forgotten he was still next to her, a fact she refused to analyze. She smiled, hoping he hadn't seen her lapse. "I know. But

please don't let it spoil such a lovely evening."
She wrapped her arms around his neck, finding it
disconcerting by half to gaze lovingly into his one
eye. She thought about kissing him, but his
tightly pursed red lips weren't very appealing.

"If he's not gone by Saturday..."

"You'll have him thrown out by the scruff of
his neck," she said. "Tossed on his ear with a
good swift kick in the pants for insurance."

Gary shook his head wearily. "I swear, sometimes I don't understand you, Maggie."

"Of course you do," she said, forcing herself to
sound light and cheerful. "I'm everything you
want in a wife, isn't that so? Capable, organized. I
know what fork to use, I can whip up a dinner
party in two hours. What's not to like?"

"Granted," he said. "But your ex-husband
staying in your guest house less than four weeks
before we're married? What are people going to
say?"

"Don't worry about it. No one's even going to
know he's there. I certainly won't tell. Besides, I'll
be so busy, I won't even see him. Now, why don't
you go check up on Van Pierson? I know you've
been wanting to talk to him all night."

Instantly, Gary's expression changed, which
was actually quite interesting. If the Phantom of
the Opera had been an accountant, she had the
feeling that's what he would have looked like. He
took her arms from around his neck with all the
care of a man removing a necktie after church. After one careless half grin, he was off in search of
Van Pierson of the Texas Piersons, worth his con-

siderable weight in oil, plus about a million crude barrels or so.

"I see the coast is clear."

Maggie spun around to see Fiona holding up a conciliatory glass of champagne.

"I ought to throttle you."

"I know. I was an idiot. I'm sorry."

"Some good sorry would have been if Gary had figured things out."

"I don't know. Maybe that wouldn't have been so awful."

"What are you talking about?" Maggie took the glass from her friend's hand as they headed back in to the party. "It would have been a disaster."

"Oh?" Fiona flicked her hair back, reminding Maggie of Cher during her television-show days. "Would it have been so bad to see Gary a little off-kilter? A little worried?"

"Pardon?"

"Oh, never mind me. I'm drunk. Or at least I'm trying to—holy mother-of-pearl, will you look at that."

Maggie followed Fiona's blatant stare. It was Spencer, sans makeup, sans cape, sans hat. Just Spencer. He looked out of place, but not because he wore a simple tailored white shirt, open at the neck, and plain black slacks. It was that he made everyone around him look like a clown. Not just the guy who'd come as Bozo, either. Everyone near him, from the mayor of Houston, all the way to the head coach of the Houston Rockets, suddenly seemed absurd in their costumes, like children playing make-believe. Spencer was the real McCoy. All man, muscle and power.

It had been five years, and just looking at him made her breathless.

"How did you ever let that man go?" Fiona asked, her voice almost worshipful.

"He let me go, remember?" she said blithely, even though the comment hit her where it hurt. She hadn't let him go. She'd chased him away with her own stupidity.

"You could have gone after him."

"What for? We were completely wrong for each other."

"I don't know. I've never seen you happier."

Maggie frowned. She didn't want to think about that. Nothing good could come of it. "Happy and deluded," she said. "It just wasn't meant to be."

"But don't you miss it? Just a little?"

"Miss what?"

Fiona sighed. "The way you were with him. The way he made you feel. I've never known a more exciting man than Spencer Daniels. Even when we were in high school, he was the most dangerous thing on two feet."

"No. I don't miss that one bit. I'm perfectly happy with my life now, and I wouldn't change it for the world."

"If you say so," Fiona said, the disbelief clear in her voice.

"I do," Maggie said. "I'm as happy as I could be." But her gaze stayed on Spencer as he moved through the crowd like a panther slinking through the brush.

Maybe if she said it out loud enough times, she would come to believe it herself.

4

THE THING WAS, she was over him.

It had taken almost five years, but she'd done it. Washed him out of her hair. Stopped thinking about him the last thing at night and the first thing in the morning. She'd given up mourning for Lent, regrets for Christmas and just to be on the safe side, anger for Yom Kippur. She'd made new choices, faced new demons, and even kept off the ten pounds.

So why did she have this awful, aching, sinking feeling in the pit of her stomach? She couldn't look at him anymore. Turning to Fiona, she groaned.

"You're not still in love with him, are you?" Fiona asked, studying her face. "I mean, it's been years. You haven't even talked about him since last winter."

Leave it to Fiona to remember that. One unguarded moment, one careless comment. Fiona had been getting over a guy. Again. And Maggie had thought it would help if she explained that the pain dulls, the need wanes. It doesn't disappear completely, but it's manageable. After her confession, Fiona had asked her the same question—if she was still in love with Spencer. Maggie had denied it then, too.

"Look at me, Maggie," Fiona commanded, taking off her half mask and putting it on the table.

Maggie couldn't. She looked at Fiona's shoes instead. The three-hundred-dollar pair she'd gotten on sale at Neiman's. The color matched her dress to perfection, but then that was Fiona, wasn't it?

"Dammit, look at me!"

Maggie pulled her gaze up and faced her friend. The one person she had never been able to lie to. No, Fiona wasn't the only one. The other was standing by the staircase, the only other guest without a mask on.

"Oh my God!"

"What?"

"You do still love him. Your eye is twitching."

Maggie put her fingers up to her right eye, frantic to stop the telltale sign she thought had disappeared along with Spencer. "I do not love him. I don't even like him."

"Oh, honey," Fiona said, touching her arm. "I'm so sorry. You seemed so happy with Gary."

"I was," she said. "I mean, I am. Nothing's changed."

"Everything's changed. Oh my heavens. You can't go through with it now."

"Go through with what?"

"The wedding. It wouldn't be right."

"Stop sounding like this is the last act of *Hamlet*. And don't look at me like that. You'll get wrinkles. I don't feel anything for Spencer Daniels, except irritation. I just wish I hadn't…"

"Wait a minute, honey. This is fate knocking you on the head. Pay attention, for your sake as well as Gary's."

Maggie couldn't respond. Her mouth didn't seem to work. Of all the silly ideas Fiona had ever had, this had to be the topper.

Fiona looked her over, and shook her head. "Well, don't say I didn't warn you."

"You're nuts," Maggie said, finally spitting out the words. "I'm very fond of Gary."

"No. You're very fond of créme brûlée. You either love Gary or you don't."

"I…love him," she said, but even to her own ears, the statement sounded weak.

"Yeah," Fiona said. "That's what I figured."

Maggie looked over at the staircase. Spencer was talking to Caroline. He looked so calm, so steady. Didn't anyone remember? Didn't he remember?

The day he'd walked out was etched in her memory so deeply, she knew every detail would be clear when she was ninety. It had been such a little thing, only meant to help. Yet he'd been so angry. His bitter words should have been enough to make her hate him, but they hadn't. In all her misery, she'd never been able to do that.

"So what are you going to do?" Fiona asked.

"Nothing. I have a wedding to plan. I can't be bothered by something as inconsequential as a visit by my ex-husband."

"I'd say Spencer was a lot of things, cookie, but inconsequential is not one of them."

"He's only here for a few days."

"Waterloo only lasted a few days, and look how that ended for Napoleon."

"This isn't a battle."

"I'm not so sure about that. It looks to me like Spencer has you surrounded on three flanks."

"You're jumping to some pretty big conclusions, Fiona. He's here to find a house. He's not here for me."

"Right. He's come back on the very night of your engagement party just because he's interested in real estate."

Maggie wanted to change the subject, to talk about anything—money, religion, violence on TV. It didn't matter, as long as it wasn't about Spencer. But just thinking his name made her glance his way again.

"Is that Janice?" Maggie asked, nodding surreptitiously at the woman who'd joined Spencer and her sister and was now draped over him like a poncho.

"Who, the chick in the Dorothy Lamour getup?" Fiona asked.

"Yeah."

"I think so. She always did have a thing for Spencer."

"Could she be any more blatant if she tried? I mean, come on. Why doesn't she just rip her sarong off and do a fertility dance in the pâté?"

"Oh, you're not interested in Spencer at all. I don't know what I was thinking." Fiona walked in front of Maggie and took her boldly by the shoulders. "Girlfriend, you've got a choice to make. Right now. If you don't, things could get awfully messy."

Maggie looked right into Fiona's eyes. She willed herself not to twitch. "I'm fine," she said. "I'm happy. I couldn't care less that he's here."

Fiona sighed. "Okay. Have it your own way. But just so you know, Dr. Gephart is out of town for the whole week."

"I do not need an appointment with your shrink."

"You will."

"I THOUGHT Ms. Tahiti was going to hula you into a spare bedroom for a minute there."

Spencer relaxed now that he was alone with Caroline again. "Janice was just being polite."

"In a pig's eye."

"So, come on, finish with your story. We're starting to look suspicious."

Caroline glanced around, and evidently decided Maggie was far enough away that she could talk freely. "I didn't do anything except send you the costume. Honest."

He lowered his head and looked at her sternly. "Come on, Caroline. It's me you're talking to."

"Okay. I might have mentioned to Dad you were coming. So shoot me."

"Why do I have the feeling Maggie isn't going to be very pleased with either of us come tomorrow?" Spencer said, stepping slightly back so that he could see both Caroline in front of him, and

Maggie behind the foyer centerpiece. "Did he happen to mention why he's letting me stay?"

Caroline shook her head, the feather in her headband quivering as if it were having a party all its own. "You know Dad. He doesn't say much. But I wouldn't get too excited about him being on your side. I think it's more about Gary than it is about you."

"What?" Spencer stepped closer to his ex-sister-in-law. "He doesn't like the fair-haired boy?"

"He likes him, I guess. But he doesn't think he's right for Maggie."

"Why not?"

"I don't know. But I'd wager it's the same reason I'm not keen on this marriage. Gary's..."

Spencer didn't need Caroline to tell him about Gary. He'd researched the man so thoroughly, he could have filled out his taxes for him.

"He's beige," Caroline said finally.

"Beige?" That's not how he would have described the man. Shrewd, yes. Hungry, oh, yes. But he had his weaknesses. He had to—a man doesn't become a partner in a law firm as big as Wendell, Bradley, Simmons and Hirsch by being Mr. Nice Guy.

Caroline nodded, and he struggled not to focus on her feather. "He's just bland, that's all. Nice, but he doesn't have your...you know. Your presence."

Spencer smiled. He really liked Caroline. She was something else he'd been sorry to lose. And he had his doubts that she'd want to keep in touch with him after this week. Not if things worked out the way he planned.

"He's obviously got something Maggie wants," he said, not wanting to tip his hand.

Caroline looked at him, her doubt making her look younger than her years. A wave of memories passed over him. He'd met her when she was fifteen. God, she'd been a cute kid. All arms and legs and giggles. She'd been crazy in love with Bon Jovi back then. By now, she must have moved on to real boyfriends. Caroline at twenty. It seemed hard to believe.

"Maybe so," she said. "But I can't imagine what. There's just no *there* there. The only time he gets excited is when he's talking about his law firm." She sighed again. "I was actually hoping you'd come here to stop her from marrying him."

He could tell she was waiting for him to confirm her suspicions. But it wasn't time to play his cards. Not yet. "Like I said before, I'm just here to look for a place to live, go to the reunion and wish Maggie well."

"Okay," she said grudgingly. "But you know where to find me if you change your mind."

"I sure do. Now go have some fun, Pocahontas. We've created enough havoc for one night."

She stood on tiptoe and gave him a kiss on the cheek. "I like you better without the makeup," she whispered. Then she headed off toward the music and Spencer was left to his own devices. He looked at Maggie again. She hadn't moved. Fiona was still standing guard, and he could see they were talking, but both of them stared at him instead of each other. He smiled, bowed slightly. It had no effect. It was as if they were watching a movie.

Time to make his next move.

He walked toward the two women, observing the byplay between them. Fiona started a retreat, which Maggie countered with a quick grab to the arm. A momentary debate, and then Fiona was off. He'd bet a week's salary she wouldn't go far, but with the music playing and the steady thrum of voices wafting through the foyer, she wouldn't be able to hear a word, no matter her vantage point.

Maggie, on the other hand, would hear very well. She squared her shoulders as he took his last steps toward her, ready for whatever he'd come to deliver.

"How very nice of you to change back to Spencer now that the damage is done," Maggie said acidly.

"Damage? What damage would that be?"

"You know perfectly well what I'm talking about. How dare you?"

She wasn't speaking loudly, but the intensity of her words made him hot. God, nothing was better than fighting with Maggie. Except, perhaps, making up.

"I wasn't the one who dragged you into the closet."

"You knew I didn't know you were you."

"I had no reason to think you didn't know I was me. Who else would I be?"

"Gary!"

"Oh, I think it's very clear I'm not Gary."

"And what's that supposed to mean?"

She'd moved closer. Close enough for him to see the sparkle in her eyes, the color on her cheek that had nothing to do with rouge. He could even feel her warm breath on his face. Feel her heat radiating toward him, teasing him. He wanted to take her in his arms, kiss her like he used to, like he had in the closet. But he couldn't. Not yet. There were still many things he had to do before that pretty reward.

"My love, you haven't changed at all."

"Don't say that."

"It was a compliment."

"I don't care how you meant it. I have changed. For the better, I might add. I'm not that naive girl you married, Spencer. I'll never be that naive again."

She might have changed in some respects. In five years, she could hardly help it. But from the moment he'd laid eyes on her, he'd seen that the fundamental Maggie was still the same. Haughty, vain, willful, spoiled. All the things that drove him mad. But she was also smart, funny, talented and as wicked as sin in the bedroom—or rather, the closet.

He looked her over carefully from top to bottom, then back up again, settling on her bodice. "You're still beautiful, Maggie. That hasn't changed at all."

"You have no right to look there. They belong to Gary now."

He laughed. "I've missed you."

"That's peachy. I'm touched. Now, why don't you just go back where you came from?"

The music from the other room swelled, and then the bandleader wished Maggie and Gary good luck on their marriage. He also announced that tonight's party had raised almost a quarter of a million dollars for the Houston women's shelters, all thanks to the bride-to-be.

Spencer was startled. He looked at her, but she was busy being congratulated by Tweedledum and Tweedledee. Perhaps Maggie had grown up. When he'd known her, she hadn't been very interested in charitable work. He'd come to realize she'd been a sheltered, spoiled girl who thought life owed her happiness. But five years can change a person.

The guests were heading out, and Spencer was glad. He was tired. It had been a long day, and a very eventful evening. Maggie had turned to him once more, although she kept glancing at the front door.

"You need to say goodbye to your guests," he said. "But we'll talk tomorrow. We have a lot of catching up to do."

Maggie took a step closer to him, and made sure he was looking into her eyes. "This isn't a game," she said. "This is my life. Don't screw things up for me, Spencer. Please."

He nodded as she hurried to find her fiancé. He almost felt guilty about being here. About what he intended to do. Almost.

It had taken him five years and a great deal of hard work to be able to come back. Through it all, her image had pushed him on. Urged him to keep going when any sane man would rest. She was the reason he got up in the morning. She was the reason he was successful beyond his wildest dreams. He couldn't leave now. Not when he had so much to tell her.

He didn't have much time, only a few days. But if everything worked the way he'd planned it, a few days would be enough.

All he wanted was to see the look on Maggie's face when she finally understood who he was. That he was all the things she was so frightened he'd never be. He wanted to see the regret. To hear her apology.

For her to remember, and then to beg him to stay.

Only then could he close the door and walk away from her for good.

AT THE FRONT DOOR, Maggie stood by Gary's side, hoping the smile on her face looked more real than it felt. It was excruciating to exchange these little pleasantries with her guests while she knew Spencer was lurking nearby. Gary was happy, at least. He'd made a lot of headway with Van Pierson. But when they were alone again, she had the feeling there was going to be another discussion about Spencer.

Why had he come back? The way he'd left, she'd felt sure she'd never see him again. She'd been too young, and he'd been...Spencer. It had only lasted a year. A wild, incredible, terrifying year. But that was long enough for it to nearly kill her when he'd walked out.

God, she was so confused, and having to shake hands and kiss cheeks and thank people was the last thing she wanted to be doing.

"It's almost over."

Maggie turned her head. Fiona was standing right behind her, and she'd whispered the words so only they could hear. "Thank God," Maggie whispered back.

"He's in the kitchen."

She didn't have to ask who Fiona meant. "Who's with him?" She turned back to the woman in front of her. Ellen, Helen, something like that.

"What a wonderful party," the woman said. "Such fun. I know you and Gary are going to have the most perfect marriage."

"I hope so," Maggie said. "I mean, yes, I know we will. Thank you." The woman moved on, but was instantly replaced by another guest whom she didn't know. Gary's friends. He had so many.

"He's with Caroline," Fiona said. "They're eating all the leftovers."

"That should keep him out of trouble."

"Who?"

Maggie looked sharply to her left. No more people stood in line. It was just Gary. His hat was a little crooked, his makeup the worse for wear. He looked as exhausted as she felt. "Nothing," she said. "No one."

"Maggie…"

He didn't finish the sentence. He didn't have to.

His disappointment was clear. This was their special night, and here she was focusing all her attention on her ex-husband.

"Gary," Fiona said, stepping between them. "I think it's time we took off that getup."

"Excuse me?"

Fiona took his hand in hers and led him toward the stairs. "You'll never get all that goop off your face without help. I have just the thing. Trust me, honey. I know makeup like you know torts."

Maggie waited until they were almost all the way to the second floor. Thank goodness for Fiona. Now, to figure out what was going on in the kitchen.

The house seemed huge as she crossed it. Scattered plates, napkins and glasses mixed with the remains of extravagant floral arrangements and table settings. The wait staff barely glanced at her in their efforts to clean up and go home. It looked like the end of a great party. No one would ever suspect that it had been peppered with illicit flirting and sex. More than that, no one she knew would ever think she was a participant! She barely believed it herself.

She had worked long and hard for her reputation as someone who not only got the job done, but did it with the grace and style of a well-bred lady. She'd almost single-handedly raised all the money that would build the newest domestic shelter, along with the more personally rewarding work as a counselor. She'd worked just as hard in her relationship with Gary, taking it slowly and cautiously so that this time she wouldn't make any mistakes. Her life was planned out: Marriage, a couple of kids, a home of her own, security. Spencer put all that at risk.

But she couldn't deny that her pulse quickened with each step. That knowing he was here, not knowing why, was exciting in a sick sort of way.

She had to make him leave. She *had* to.

By the time she reached the kitchen, she was almost running. Jerking to a stop in front of the door, she composed herself, willing her heart to slow down, her face to relax into easy confidence, her hair to behave. She had the urge to tear the extensions out, but the thought of what that would do stopped her. Now would not be the time to look like the Wild Woman of Borneo.

Spencer's laughter wafted through the door. Rich, low, unique. She'd have recognized the sound anywhere. She'd fallen in love with that sound, and when it stopped, it had left a hole inside her. Now, hearing it again after so many years, after building up the wall inside her brick by brick, sent a shock wave through her. The wall trembled, but it didn't break. She wouldn't let it break.

Pushing open the door, she walked into the kitchen prepared to meet her nemesis head-on. Activity swirled around her. Dishes clanked, water ran, shoes clicked on the tile, a cacophony that seemed to pulse at her temples. *He* was at the round breakfast table, sitting with Caroline and their mother. Calm and serene, he leaned back in his chair, arm casually flung over the back of Caroline's, as if the buzz and scurry wouldn't dare bother the likes of him. A Lilliputian banquet was spread before them—tiny quiches, miniature crab cakes, silver dollar–size blini topped with caviar. Caroline and Spencer each had a glass of champagne, and Mother had a cup of tea.

They all looked up at her at the same time and, in that second, she saw Caroline's excitement, Mother's anger and Spencer's confidence. A beat later, her mother and sister pasted on bright smiles that revealed little. But Spencer didn't try to mask anything.

"Where's the man of the hour?" he asked.

"Fiona took him upstairs to help him take off his makeup."

Spencer stood and pulled out the chair next to him. "Join us," he said, as if it were *his* house, *his* relatives, *his* food. He'd changed. Not only his body and the way his shoulders had broadened, but the inner confidence she'd once seen only in the bedroom was now as natural to him as his easy smile. Just as she wasn't a kid any longer, neither was he. Looking at him, standing so calm while the bustle swirled around him, she really understood that he was a man now. A formidable man.

"I'm exhausted," she said. "I think I'm just going to find Gary and say good-night."

"Sure you don't want a snack first?"

"No," she said. "I've had enough."

Spencer stepped away from the table. "I'll walk you."

She almost said no, but there were a few things she wanted to say to him privately. She went to her mother and leaned down to kiss her cheek. "Thank you for tonight. It was wonderful."

"I'm glad you had a good time," her mother said. "And don't you let him bamboozle you," she whispered.

"Don't worry," Maggie whispered back. "I've got everything under control."

Spencer was at her shoulder, and as she turned he put his hand on the small of her back. She felt the shiver all the way up her spine and moved so quickly to break the contact that she almost knocked over a platter of empty glasses.

"Careful," he said, reaching out and touching her again.

The shiver wasn't quite as bad this time, but it was still there. As soon as they cleared the hurdle of the center island, she stepped aside, dislodging his hand.

Once they were in the dining room, the noise abated and she felt as though she could think again. It was the perfect time to talk to Spencer. Gary would be coming down in a minute, so nothing could happen. She stopped at the base of the stairs and turned on him. "What are you doing here, Spencer?"

"I told you."

"Yeah, yeah. But what are you really doing here?"

He gave her an appraising look, but she knew him well enough to know that was just a delaying tactic while he decided what to tell her. She crossed her arms impatiently.

"A lot has changed since I left."

"I know. I got over you, for one thing."

The corners of his lips quirked up, as if her comment was amusing, but nothing to be taken seriously. "I didn't get over you."

The words hit her like a blow. She had to grab the banister to steady herself, while she struggled to keep her expression neutral. She'd never expected to hear him say that. She'd convinced herself that once he walked away, he'd never given her a second thought. That he'd been so disappointed with her that he'd never want to see her again. Knowing that had made her strong, had colored all her decisions. And now he said it wasn't true? She wasn't going to let him know how shaken she was. Not tonight. Not at her engagement party.

"That's too bad," she said lightly, as if the world hadn't just tilted sideways.

"We'll see."

"No, we won't. Whatever little game you're playing, you can stop right now. I'm with Gary. I'm going to stay with Gary."

"Why?"

"Because he's the right man for me."

Spencer took a step closer toward her. It was too close. She saw too much, felt the heat from his body. But her back was against the staircase, and she'd have to push him away to move.

"He's not the right man, Maggie. He's just the safe man."

Welcome anger strengthened her knees, helped her breathe again. "And what's wrong with that? Don't you think I deserve to be safe?"

He shook his head. "You've had safe your whole life. You've only taken one big risk, and that was when you married me. It changed everything. How you looked, what you tried, how you felt about yourself. You've never been better than that and you know it."

"You have an amazingly selective memory. I've never been more miserable than when I was with you, and I don't intend to ever be that miserable again."

He winced as if she'd slapped him. But the next instant he looked so cool, so very in control, she thought maybe she'd imagined his reaction.

"Miserable, huh? That's not what I remember. What I remember were the nights. The long nights, and all that heat."

"Stop it. Don't even start to go there. We're adults. Surely we can be civilized."

"Civilized? That wasn't what you wanted from me, ever." He leaned forward, grasping her arm tightly. "Or is that something you've forgotten, too?" he whispered, his voice a low, feral growl filled with steamy nights and tangled sheets, her body trembling and crying out for more.

She broke from his grasp, forcing distance between them. "It doesn't matter what I wanted back then. What I want now is for you to go. Leave me be."

"I'm not going anywhere."

Looking at him, she knew he was telling her the truth. He wasn't going to leave until he was ready. Nothing could make him go, not her parents, not the sheriff, not anything. When Spencer

made up his mind, that was that. No debates.
When he wanted something, he got it. She knew,
because a long time ago, he'd wanted her. "Fine.
Stay. But listen to me, Spencer. I don't feel anything for you. Nothing. The fire is dead, and it has
been for a long time."

"I'd believe you if it wasn't for one thing."

"What's that?"

He leaned over, his lips a scant inch from her
ear. *"You knew it was me in the closet."*

5

SPENCER KEPT his gaze on her face. If he was off the mark, he'd know it quickly. Her eyes widened and her lips parted. He could hear her sharp intake of breath. The pink came to her cheeks then spread, making her look flushed. No, he wasn't off the mark. He'd hit the bull's-eye.

He leaned forward to kiss her. To remind her again that she'd known his taste, his scent, just as he'd known hers. But just as his lips brushed hers, he heard Fiona's voice above them. He pulled back. This wasn't the time.

Maggie's chest rose and fell rapidly, and from where he stood it presented a very nice view. It was nice to know he could still make her hyperventilate.

He stepped farther back, giving her more room. It was late, and he didn't want a scene. She looked up the stairs, then back at him. He could see her turmoil, her struggle to gather her wits. He'd made his point. No reason to make her suffer more tonight.

He smiled at Gary, hoping Maggie would get the signal that, for the moment, at least, he wasn't going to cause trouble. Spencer took the opportunity to get his first good look at Gary. He was

handsome, nothing remarkable, but his background was there on his face. He'd come from
money, just like Maggie. He looked as if he hadn't
missed a day at the golf course in his life.

"I see Betty's had the staff working overtime,"
Gary said, his voice friendly, but not friendly
enough to disguise a note of suspicion.

"They're all busy in the kitchen," Spencer said.
"I was just on my way to the guest house. It's
been a long day."

"Great then." Gary moved next to Maggie and
put his arm around her waist. "If you need any
help with the real estate issue, give me a call. I've
got several good people."

"Thanks. But I've got it covered. Congratulations again, you two." He turned to Fiona. "How
would you like to escort me, beautiful?"

Fiona nodded, then looked over at Maggie and
Gary. Something changed in her face, small, sub-
tle, but real. A sadness, an ennui. What was that
about? Then she kissed her hosts, and faced him.
"I'm all yours, gorgeous."

"The evening just keeps getting better," he
said, taking her hand in his. But before he had a
chance to lead her away, Maggie turned to Gary
in a very broad move, one she intended him to
witness. She smiled as if she wanted Gary to see
her back molars, then took both his hands in hers.
"I'm so happy about tonight," she said, her voice
bouncing off the walls like a handball. "It was just
perfect." Then she kissed him. Hard. She even
moved her hand in back of his head to steady
him. It was a theatrical kiss, with all the appropri-

ate sound effects. But it didn't work. It was all for
show. All to prove a point that had already been
undermined.

"So, are we going to stand around and watch
them smooch, or are we going to put you to bed?"

"Fiona, I've missed you."

"Yeah, right." She started across the foyer,
pulling him along.

He didn't look back, even though he was curious as to how long Maggie could hold the clench.
Let her think she'd won the round. It made no difference in the grand scheme of things.

Fiona slowed as they headed toward the back
door. "You gonna tell me what you're doing back
here, or are you going to make me wait to hear it
from Maggie?"

"I'm here looking for a house. Thought I'd
check out the reunion as long as I'm here. That's
all."

"Please, Spence. It's me you're talking to." She
reached the door and opened it for him. The
warm, humid air hit him way before he stepped
outside.

It was true. Fiona wasn't someone he could
fool. She never had been. Even back in high
school, long before Maggie had given him a second look, Fiona had been a friend. She'd never
minded that he wasn't part of her crowd. She'd
accepted him on his own terms, and it was her, in
the end, who'd convinced Maggie she should go
out with him.

He put his arm around her shoulder, and gave

her a squeeze. "Okay. I'll tell you, but you have to tell me some things first."

"Like?"

"I want to hear about Gary."

"He's engaged. And he's not your type."

"God, I've dreamed of that wit on long, lonely nights."

"I wish. All right. I'll tell you about Gary, but first let's go sit down. My feet are killing me."

They walked past the Olympic-size pool, the azalea bushes and the gazebo. The guest house looked exactly as it had five years ago. A pretty little cottage complete with a front porch. The key was under the mat, as always, and the moment he walked in it was as if he'd gone back in time.

The elegant, lush decor was Maggie's touch, not her mother's. Thick pile carpeting, dark hunter green. An overstuffed couch and ottoman. Chintz chairs. The incredible Lorrain prints on the pale green walls. And of course, plants—lots of them. Even the smell was the same—lemon and spice. He'd always associated that scent with Maggie.

Fiona walked past him to the little kitchen and got some orange juice from the fridge. She poured herself a glass. "You want one?"

He shook his head, still noticing the little things around him that had once been in another apartment long ago, like the teak telephone stand, the bookcase he'd gotten her for her birthday, the Baccarat crystal vase on the mantel.

"Déjà vu, huh?" Fiona asked as she slid off her shoes and walked barefoot to the couch. Hiking up her long dress until her thighs were uncovered, she sat down, curling her legs beneath her.

He nodded. "It's been a long time." He went to the big chair next to where Fiona sat, and settled in. A wave of exhaustion hit him, and he realized just how stressful the night had been. He needed to sleep for about a hundred years. But that would have to wait. "Tell me about him, Fiona. About how he is with Maggie."

She sighed. "He's a great guy. Not great like you, but great. He wants success, and he works for it, but he doesn't mow down everyone in his path. In fact, he does more *pro bono* work than most lawyers I've known."

"Okay, but what about him and Maggie?"

"They work well together. You know how organized she is, and he needs someone like that. She likes that he's steady and reliable."

"Sounds like they should open an office together, not get married."

"Maggie cares for him, and I know he cares for her."

"Cares? I care for my secretary, it doesn't mean I want her as my wife."

"So I'm right. You *do* want her back. Wow. That's amazing."

"Oh no. Don't misinterpret my interest. I don't want Maggie back. And I can assure you, she doesn't want me."

Fiona made a most unladylike sound. "Sure."

He gave her a look that most people had the good sense to interpret as a warning. Fiona laughed.

"If you don't want her back, what are doing here?"

"I'm opening up new corporate offices here. I'm not that kid who left Houston with a hundred bucks in his worn-out pocket."

"I know. I've been paying attention."

"Really?"

She nodded. "It hasn't been difficult. You've been in the papers."

"Only the financial papers."

"I may look like I don't know a prospectus from a potato pie, but believe me, I take my finances very seriously."

"I don't doubt it for a moment. You're one of the shrewdest people I know."

"So don't try to con me about your interests. You're here for one thing—to get Maggie back."

He frowned. "I will admit that I came here for more than just the office."

Fiona looked at him in a way that was unsettling. No one seemed to look at him that way anymore. They were either too intimidated or too concerned with their own agendas. But she had nothing to fear or gain from him.

"I didn't want her to forget."

"You? Don't be stupid."

He smiled. Only Fiona.

"Breaking a woman's heart has a strange way of making a lasting impression. You know, she really loved you. She didn't mean to hurt you."

He leaned forward. "You don't think I had a right to be upset?"

Fiona shook her head. "I know you two were

crazy in love, more in love than anyone I've ever seen. She did the best she could. You should have stuck around and worked it out."

Now it was his turn to shake his head. "No. I couldn't. Fiona, she didn't want what she had. She wanted something else, to make me something else. Someone who'd fit in her life."

"She just didn't know any better."

"Right. She needed to grow up. So did I."

"And now you're back. Maybe to show off your new company a little? Your new, high-powered friends?"

"That's part of it."

"What's the rest?" she asked.

He could see her concern. She was Maggie's closest friend, and no matter what her feelings were toward him, Maggie was her first priority. He didn't want to worry Fiona. But there were certain things he had to do.

He stood up. "It's late."

Fiona took the hint and stood up, too. She walked over to him and took both his hands in hers. "I'd be careful if I were you, Spencer. You're playing with big weapons here, and people could get hurt."

"You really think I could hurt her?"

She squeezed his hands hard. "Don't play games with me. You know what you do to her, how vulnerable she is. Listen to me, Spencer. Revenge might look good on paper, but it's not the way to go. You won't get any satisfaction from it."

"Revenge? Is that what you think I'm here for, Fiona?"

She nodded. "I think you were hurt. I think you're still hurt."

"Five years is a long time. People grow up."

"Sometimes."

"All I want is some closure. I'm going to be living in Houston, and I'm going to run into Maggie. We left things unfinished."

"Fine. Closure is good. As long as it doesn't make things worse. Be careful, honey. Don't get her all tangled up in the past."

He nodded.

She leaned forward and kissed his cheek. Then she let him go, and walked to the door.

"Fiona?"

She waited.

"He's not right for her."

"You don't know that."

"Yes I do. And I think you know it, too."

She turned, and walked slowly back to where he was standing. "I love her. And if Gary makes her happy, then that's good enough for me."

"Happy? Is that what she is?"

"She's comfortable. You know that's important to her."

"It wasn't always."

"It's true, there isn't a lot of passion between them. But that's one of the things she likes about him. She's frightened of that kind of passion."

"Frightened," he repeated, thinking about what she'd told him. Not welcoming the doubt that preyed on his mind.

"Just be very sure that you know what you're getting into. You're a smart man, Spencer. So be smart."

MAGGIE WATCHED Gary get into his BMW, then she shut the front door and leaned her forehead on the cool wood. What a night. What a nightmare. Gary knew something was wrong, although she couldn't imagine that he'd guessed what she'd done with Spencer in the closet. Who would? It wasn't like her at all, at least not the woman she'd become. Years ago, doing something that wild, that uninhibited, wouldn't have been so out of character for her, but she'd grown up. Gotten wise. And careful.

She blamed it all on the champagne. It had to be the champagne. From this day forward, she wasn't ever going to drink the stuff again. That was a promise.

Clearly, she was still under the influence. If she were sober, the idea of Spencer in the guest house wouldn't bother her in the least. Well, maybe it would, but not in the way it bothered her now.

For years she'd worked hard at banishing him from her thoughts. Forgetting what he'd meant to her, and how it had all ended so horribly. She'd thrown herself into her fund-raising work, dedicated herself to being a good fiancée. She'd re-created herself into the woman she was supposed to be, and she'd put the past behind her. Now she realized all of her hard work had been for nothing. Old feelings, fresh and crisp as if no time had passed, swirled inside her, the memories jumbled and haphazard, yet so clear each one was a punch in the stomach.

That wasn't what bothered her the most, though. The bad feelings, the old hurts, were at least familiar. What had her so worried were the other memories. The good ones. The feeling of love so strong that it threatened to knock the wind out of her lungs. The excitement that had always accompanied Spencer, that made her pulse race and her eyes search for him in every crowd, in every empty room. The tightness in her stomach, and the way she felt the need to squeeze her legs together at the sound of his name.

He'd come back and tangled her up in a mess of feelings she'd never wanted again. She should just walk out there right now and tell him to leave. To never come back. Except…

Dammit, she *had* known it was him in the closet. Not by name. She would have stopped if she'd been that aware. Something deep inside had recognized him for who he was. Her body had reacted to his touch as if he'd never been away. All he'd done was rekindle a flame that had never completely died out.

Just thinking about it, her body betrayed her again. She felt tight, anxious. All the old feelings she'd had when she'd wanted Spencer all the time. When they hadn't been able to keep their hands off each other, not for anything. God, she thought she'd purged that part of her!

She closed her eyes, and the rush of sense memories nearly swept her away. The way he'd taken her as if he owned her. She could almost feel his hands as they moved up her thighs. The way he knew how to kiss her, how to touch her. Making love to Spencer was like taking a drug. It robbed her of logic, of reason. And left her needing more and more.

But that didn't mean she still loved him. She couldn't love a man who'd hurt her the way he had. Who didn't understand her at all—at least, not anymore. It would be insane to let Spencer into her life again.

"Maggie, you're still up?"

She turned to see her father, now out of his absurd costume, wearing his familiar dark blue robe and slippers. He held a glass of milk, which she knew was meant for her mother. "Not for long, Dad. I don't even think I have the energy to get out of this getup."

"Okay, then. Sleep well."

Maggie touched his arm. "I'd like to ask you something."

"Yes?"

"Why are you being so nice to Spencer?"

Her father frowned. "Let's sit down." He led her to the dining-room table. The room was remarkably clean considering all that had gone on tonight. But she could still hear the clatter from the kitchen. She ignored that and turned to her father.

"I know he hurt you," he said. "But I also know you hurt him."

Maggie shook her head. "No, he—"

"Honey? I know it's not pleasant, but it's also

not right to keep blaming him. You had a part in this."

Her stomach clenched. He wasn't telling her anything new. He'd said the same thing five years ago, but she hadn't listened then. "It was one stupid mistake. Spencer's reaction was completely out of proportion."

"All a man really has is his pride," Frank said softly. "You took that away from him."

Maggie couldn't speak for a moment. The lump in her throat was too big. She knew her father was right. It was just that...God, she didn't want him to think less of her. Not him. Her father had always been there for her. He'd always let her know that she was cherished. All she'd ever wanted was to make him proud, but he wasn't proud of her about this.

She met his gaze and saw such affection that she couldn't stop her tears. Despite everything, he still loved her. "I'm sorry I disappointed you."

He reached over and squeezed her hand. "I love you. I'm proud of you. You've grown into a wonderful woman. All the work you do for those poor women. The way you care so much for others. But this business with Spencer isn't going to go away. It's time for you to face him. That's why I let him stay. For you to talk to him. To apologize."

"He walked out on me, remember?" she said, still hanging on to the one thought that had gotten her through all of it. "Not the other way around."

Frank shook his head and put his hand on hers.

"I didn't raise you to run away from your mistakes. You lied about him. You tried to make him into something he wasn't."

"I thought it would help," she said, but even she could hear the weakness in her voice.

"In what way? People check up on résumés, Maggie. You know that. If he'd been caught in those lies, it could have ruined his whole future."

"Dad, I just wanted to help him get a job. He was so desperate, and it's not like I said he was a doctor or anything. What difference would it have made if people thought he went to Wharton instead of the University of Texas? And you would have given him the recommendation."

"I would have, but that's not the point. What you did was make him feel that he wasn't good enough for you. That you were embarrassed by his background. That's why he left. Not the piece of paper."

Maggie's insides churned. Her face heated and she wanted to run. This was awful. She loved her father so much, and for him to be so ashamed...

"Margaret, you made a mistake. We all do that. But you never made it right. You have that chance now. Make it right with Spencer."

"Even if I do say I'm sorry, it won't change anything."

"It will. It will change you. It'll give you back something you've lost."

"What?"

"Your pride."

That was it. The pressure built in her chest until she thought she would burst. She turned away from her father, not wanting him to see. It was a long time until she could breathe normally again. Until she wiped her face dry with the back of her hand.

When she turned back, he smiled at her. "You know, Spencer might not have been the right man for you to have married, and I still contend you were too young, but in a lot of ways, he was good for you."

"Good for me?" she asked, her voice still choked with emotion.

"Yes. You were never so happy, and never so willing to take on life's challenges as you were with him."

"Daddy, you were right the first time. I was too young, too naive. I didn't understand much of anything back then."

"And now that you understand so much, are you happier?"

"Happier?" She thought for a moment, and what came to mind was her work. But something crucial was missing. Some key that she'd had once, but had lost. "I don't know about that. I am saner. By a lot."

"I suppose that has merits."

Maggie squeezed her father's hand and sighed. He was right. It was time she faced Spencer and closed that chapter of her life. "I'll tell him I'm sorry. I do owe him that much. But nothing more, Dad. I can't— I won't risk that kind of pain again. Not even if that makes you ashamed."

His gaze grew tender and his eyes shone with the hint of tears. "Right now, I couldn't be prouder of you." He cleared his throat and sat back on his chair. "Well, this milk is getting cool. Your mother won't like that."

She nodded. "Thanks, Dad."

"You're welcome. Now, go get some sleep."

She stood up as he did, and she watched him walk toward his room. He'd changed in the last few years. His hair had gotten whiter—at least what was left of it. His spare tire had grown and his step had slowed. But he was still her hero. He always would be.

Maggie got up and headed for the stairs. With a great deal of effort, she made it to her bedroom and managed to take off her clothes and slip on a nightshirt before she sat down heavily on the bed. Without the aid of a mirror, she took off her hairpieces, then dragged a brush through her own poor tresses.

All she had to do now was take off her makeup, and then she could sleep. She could stop thinking. Feeling. God, she longed for an escape.

When she finally crawled into bed, she thought about the task in front of her. Apologizing to Spencer wasn't going to be easy. But, for the first time in years, she felt oddly at peace.

HE SAT in her seat at the breakfast table.

He drank his coffee from her favorite cup.

He read her section of the newspaper.

Dammit.

She walked right past him, straight into the kitchen. She didn't even say good-morning to her parents or Caroline. All she wanted was strong black coffee and about a hundred aspirins.

Cora, the woman who'd taken care of the house since Maggie was seven, stood by the coffeepot. She'd left the party to the caterers. Her job description didn't include parties over ten people. From the scowl on her face, Maggie could see she was not pleased with the way the caterers had left things.

"They broke three plates," she said, not bothering with a good-morning. "They scratched the floor and they left a pile of cigarette butts outside the door."

"I'm sorry, Cora. But they did do a good job last night."

"I hope so." Cora, in her pale blue uniform and thick white hospital shoes, poured Maggie a cup of coffee, then handed it to her. "I see he's back."

"Yes, he is," Maggie said, taking the cup gratefully. "Surprise."

"Some surprise. What's he want?"

"He says he's looking for a house."

"He won't find one in the dining room."

"I suppose he means to go out with a real estate agent later today."

"Does your intended know he's here?"

"Gary and he met last night."

"Hmm. And what did Gary say?"

"He was very gracious."

"Well, I smell trouble."

"Cora, I'm surprised at you," a deep voice interrupted. "Trouble? Me?"

Maggie whirled around to see the man in question standing at the kitchen door. Her first thought was how elegant he was. How he, more than she, looked as if he belonged here. In his khaki slacks, his beige polo shirt and with his hair slightly damp, he was the picture of a well-heeled gentleman. No one would ever guess he'd grown up in a housing project.

Cora "hmmphed," but when Maggie glanced at her, she could see the hint of a smile on the older woman's pale face. So much for smelling trouble.

"Hello, Cora, my love."

She didn't answer him.

He went behind her and slipped her a kiss on the cheek. "I've missed you, sweetheart."

She "hmmphed" again, but Maggie knew she was eating up the attention. Cora had always had a soft spot for Spencer, even though she'd go to her death denying it.

He laughed, then turned around. "Maggie," he said, walking toward her, "I've got a proposition for you."

"No."

"You haven't heard what it is yet."

"Doesn't matter. The answer is no."

"I can see I should have waited until after you had your coffee," he said, grinning.

"Caffeine is not the problem. You are. Why aren't you out looking for houses?"

"That's part of my proposition. I want you to come with me."

"Why?"

"For several reasons. One, I respect your judgment. Two, you know River Oaks well, and three, I want to talk."

"About what?"

"What do you think? It's been a long time. We have some unfinished business."

Her father's words from last night came crashing down on her. Spencer wanted his apology. She wouldn't be able to look at her dad if she didn't make it right. It wouldn't be easy, though. Not just because she'd have to tell Spencer she was sorry. But because she was already reacting to his closeness with a pounding heart and tension that made her squeeze muscles she had no business squeezing. And she hadn't even had her coffee.

Dammit.

ment. Two you know Ryan Oakwell, and does

6

"MAGGIE, I think you'd better come out here," her
mother called from the dining room.

Spencer held her gaze for one more second,
then she broke free and called back, "I'll be right
there."

Before she could move, Spencer touched her
arm. Softly. Just his hand on her sleeve. No pressure at all. But the touch set off a chain reaction
she was completely helpless to stop. A quick frisson shot up to her shoulder, then down her back,
infiltrating her insides until every inch of her ac-
knowledged his power to change her. It wasn't
fair. It wasn't supposed to be. She should have
been immune.

He looked at her with furrowed eyebrows, and
then he smiled with such satisfaction that she
knew he knew what he'd done to her. She pulled
back with a jerk, spilling coffee on the floor. Without looking at him for even one more second, she
stepped past him toward the kitchen door. Hating that the impression of his hand lingered on
her arm, she concentrated on not spilling more of
her coffee—a Herculean task with him following
so close on her heels.

"You have a phone call," her mother said, eyeing Spencer suspiciously.

"Who is it?" Not that it mattered. Maggie was just grateful for the distraction. Although she wasn't quite back to normal yet. She doubted she would be until Spencer left for good.

"Darlene."

Maggie put her cup down on the table. The linen was back in place, the floral centerpiece a new one, borrowed from last night's party. Her mother had her one poached egg on toast, and her glass of orange juice, which helped calm Maggie's nerves. Some things never changed.

Walking over to the phone on the sideboard, she wondered if Darlene's call had to do with the party last night, or if she just had more questions about the wedding. As a wedding consultant, Darlene couldn't be doing a more professional job, even though she seemed a little too excitable given the emotional nature of her job.

As Maggie took the telephone, she glanced down at the newspaper sitting next to the crystal candy dish. It was the entertainment section, where they posted social announcements. Only this time, she and the two Phantoms were on the front page. Thank God she'd set down her coffee, or she would have spilled it all over the Persian rug.

"Hello?" she squeaked, picking up the paper and staring at the picture.

"Is it off?"

"Pardon?" Maggie could hardly believe it. It was an awful picture. Her face looked as if she'd just seen a ghost, and the two Phantoms appeared to be on the brink of pummeling each other. The body of the article appeared tame enough. Just a rather bland rundown of who had been at the party. But the picture wasn't your ordinary pre-wedding snapshot. Then she looked at the caption. They'd gotten the names wrong. They had her marrying Spencer.

"The wedding. Is it off? I've already sent out the invitations. The caterers have placed their orders. And the flowers! Oh, God."

Maggie barely heard Darlene's breathy voice. She stared at the picture, at the caption, then the picture again. They had her marrying Spencer! What was Gary going to say? What about his law partners? Not to mention all her friends at the shelters, and all the women from Mother's Save the Bayou committee and then there was everyone from the symphony. Most of them knew she'd been married before, and even though she'd taken back her maiden name, by now they'd probably all heard Spencer was really her ex-husband. She could practically hear the phone lines buzzing with the gossip.

It was all Spencer's fault. What the hell was he thinking, coming back into her life? Pretending he was Gary—fooling her in the closet. *The closet.* At the thought, the frisson was back, only this time, it made her hand shake so much she dropped the newspaper.

"Maggie? Hello? Are you there? Is the wedding off?"

"Nothing's off, Darlene," Maggie said, turning

around so Spencer wasn't even in her peripheral vision. "The wedding is going on as planned. Where did you get the idea it wouldn't?"

"From the *Chronicle*. It said you're marrying someone named Spencer Daniels."

"It's a mistake. An error. Nothing more."

"Gary sure didn't seem to think so. I talked to him this morning. I needed to find out about his groomsmen. We're having some trouble with the tuxedos, and I told him that Tim Braddock needed to come in for another fitting—"

"Darlene! What did Gary say?"

"Oh. Well, gosh. He seemed upset."

Maggie fought the panic filling her chest. "Trust me, Darlene. The wedding is going on as planned. *Nothing is wrong!*" She looked at the table, at Spencer sitting so calmly eating his bacon as if he were completely blameless. Then her gaze shifted to her mother, whose mouth pursed so tightly, Maggie thought she might break.

"Don't yell at me," Darlene said. "I'm not the one who made the mistake."

"You're right," Maggie said, forcing herself to calm down. "I'm the one who made the mistake. Not you."

"Okay, then. We'll talk again this afternoon."

Maggie hung up the phone and turned to Spencer. "Thanks again for popping in last night." She picked up the paper and tossed it to him.

"We'll make sure the error is corrected," her mother said, her agitation making her voice quiver. Being the proper Southern lady she was bred to be prevented from saying what she really thought, at least in front of anyone who wasn't family. And Spencer was no longer family.

"No? Not only does it look like I'm marrying the wrong man, it looks like a publicity photo for World Wide Wrestling."

"Come on, Maggie. It's just a picture," Spencer said. He patted the chair next to him. "Sit down, eat some breakfast. It'll help your headache."

"How do you know I have a headache?"

He smiled. "Just a guess."

"Do me a favor. Stop guessing."

"What happened to that famous sense of humor of yours?"

"You. You're what happened to it."

He patted the chair seat again. "Juice. Eggs. Toast. Don't those sound yummy?"

"Quit it. I have to call Gary."

Just then Caroline breezed into the room. "No, you don't. He phoned to say he's on his way over."

"Oh, God." Maggie rubbed her aching temples, wondering if anyone had ever died of a hangover. Perhaps, if she were lucky, she'd be the first. She glared at her little sister. "I thought you went after that reporter last night."

"I did."

"So how did that picture get in there?"

"I went after him. I didn't say I caught him."

"Great. Wonderful."

"Cheer up, Maggie. It'll really liven up your wedding-memory album."

"Oh, that just makes everything okay."

"Sheesh. What a grump. What's for breakfast?"

Caroline flounced past Maggie and sat down in the seat Spencer had saved for *her*. Looking entirely headache free, Caroline dished herself up a plateful of scrambled eggs and hash-brown potatoes.

Maggie sighed, turned and headed for the stairs. She'd just climb back into bed and sleep until tomorrow. Surely by then Spencer would be gone, Gary would be on his business trip to New York, Darlene would be knee-deep in corsages and she wouldn't feel as though the Kodo drum troupe were rehearsing in her head.

"Maggie?" her mother called. "Where are you going?"

She didn't answer. Halfway up the stairs, the doorbell rang. It was Gary. He could have her breakfast. She just kept on climbing. Bed. It sounded so peaceful.

"MAGGIE?"

She heard Spencer's whisper, but she didn't pull the covers down from over her head. If she lay perfectly still, maybe he'd go away.

He didn't.

She felt the dip of the bed, then his hand on her hip. She willed herself to block the shiver that was becoming far too familiar at his touch. She *wouldn't* let him get to her.

"Honey? I'm sorry you didn't have a pretty picture in the paper. And that they got the names mixed up. I'll call. I promise. They'll print a correction in tomorrow's paper."

She sniffed. Then she heard the door open again.

"I'll take it from here," Gary said.

The bed shifted again as Spencer stood up. Then it dipped once more.

"Honey?"

Gary. His hand touched her on the exact same spot on her hip. Nothing happened. No quiver. No shiver. Nothing.

"I'm sorry about all this. I've talked to the attorneys at the paper. They're going to correct their mistake tomorrow. And I've told them to run another picture. Of just the two of us. Oh, and I called Mother."

She slowly pulled the covers down, just to her nose. Gary, in his Brooks Brothers suit and silk tie, looked more perturbed than his gentle words had led her to believe. But he wasn't looking at her. He was staring at Spencer, who leaned oh-so-casually against her dresser.

"Gary," she said.

He didn't turn.

"Gary!"

He looked at her and his mouth seemed to struggle between a scowl and a smile. The smile won. "Hi," he said. "Ready to come out?"

She shook her head no.

Gary sighed very quietly, then took a quick glance at his watch. "All right," he said. "What would you like me to do?"

"Nothing," she said. It came out muffled from underneath her quilt. She pulled the cover down to her chin. "Nothing. I know you have a plane to catch. I'm fine."

"You don't look fine."

"I have a little headache. It's nothing."

"Your mother said… Maybe you should go to see your doctor, huh?"

"I don't need a doctor. I need some sleep."

Gary looked at Spencer again. "I thought you were going to look at houses?"

"I am. My real estate lady will be here in an hour."

Gary looked at his watch again.

"Gary," she said, "go. Everything's fine."

"I'm not in any rush."

"I don't want to be responsible for you having a stroke. I know how you hate to wait until the last minute. So go."

"But…"

"He's going to be gone all day. It's not an issue."

Gary studied her for a long while, then looked at Spencer.

"I'm not an issue," Spencer said. "Honest."

"What about the next two days?" Gary said. "I won't be back until Tuesday."

"I have too much to do to worry about him," she said. "I've got a wedding to prepare, remember?"

Gary, still staring at Spencer, frowned so deeply Maggie thought his chin would crack. "Okay, then. I'll call you," he said.

"Thanks," Spencer said. "That means a lot to me."

"He meant me," Maggie said, tossing off the quilt and climbing out of bed. She hadn't changed, but she had taken her shoes off. Her slacks were fine, but the blouse was all wrinkled. She'd have to change. For now, she slipped the pumps back on and went to her dresser, ignoring Spencer completely. She brushed her hair, pulling it back into a barrette. When she turned to face the men again, Gary was right there. She gasped, not expecting him to be so close, or to look so fierce. He never looked at her like that. The only time she'd seen this expression was when he was up against a particularly canny lawyer. Then she got it. The face, the closeness, the way his hands clenched, they were all for Spencer's benefit. It was clear Spencer brought out the passion in Gary far more than she did. Maybe they should take Spencer along on the honeymoon.

Gary grasped her arms and kissed her abruptly on the mouth. Actually, he missed and hit some of her mouth and some of her cheek. Then he squeezed her arms, looked at his watch, scowled at Spencer and walked out the door.

Maggie faced her ex, and gave him a scowl of her own. "I have to change. Do you mind?"

He shook his head. "Not at all."

"I meant, get out."

"It's not like I haven't seen you in your underwear before."

"You lost that privilege quite some time ago. Now excuse me," she said. Without another glance, she turned away, walked into her closet and started to unbutton her blouse. She expected

to hear the door close, and that's what happened.
Except it wasn't the door to her room. It was the
closet door, and Spencer was on the wrong side of
it.

"What are you doing?"

He smiled, his gaze moving to her hand, which
rested on the fourth button of her blouse. "I
thought we could talk. Now that we have some
privacy."

"Spencer, knock it off. Let me get dressed. I'll
see you downstairs."

"Right," he said. "I don't get to watch anymore." His hand went to the light switch and the
next instant they were in the dark.

"Spencer!"

"God, I love being in closets with you," he said,
only his voice was closer now. "I never realized it
until last night."

She felt afraid, although not for her safety.
Afraid that he was so near, and that she felt his
heat. Closets. She shouldn't go into closets. Ever.
"That was a mistake," she said, making sure she
didn't reveal the jumpiness she felt.

"Pulling me into the closet was a mistake," he
said. "Staying for the duration wasn't."

She backed up, almost losing her balance on a
pair of shoes, but then his hands were on her
shoulders, steadying her. Before she could regain
her equilibrium, he pulled her toward him until
her body pressed against his from shoulder to
knee.

Her outrage at his boldness didn't seem to ex-
tend to her body. Instantly, she was acutely aware

of her breasts pressing on his chest, and the way her nipples hardened. She found herself moving against him, struggling, but to get away? Or to feel her thighs against his?

"You knew it was me, didn't you?" he said, brushing his lips against her ear. Making her tremble.

"No. I thought you were Gary."

"Liar."

"Stop it. Please, Spencer."

"I'm not holding you tight."

"You are. Your hands…"

He let her go. But he didn't move back. Her mind told her to step away, to stop this right now. She was engaged to another man. Spencer wasn't hers anymore—he never would be again. And yet it was like being held in a magnetic field, the laws of attraction working overtime.

Another moment passed, him so still and quiet that all she could hear was her own heartbeat.

Then his fingers found her chin, and he tilted up her head. She opened her mouth to tell him to stop, but he kissed her silent.

She groaned at his taste, at the feel of his lips. Of course she'd known it was him last night. He'd awakened her, like Sleeping Beauty, from five years of denying her own needs. From convincing herself that what she'd felt with him wasn't real, but only the exaggerated memories of a girl who was too young to know better.

But now she did know better. It hadn't been her imagination. He really did make her feel completely alive, utterly wanton, like a primal female in heat. She changed in his arms.

"Oh, dammit, Maggie," he said, releasing her from his kiss, only to take her captive with his hands as they moved fiercely down her back. "Why the hell couldn't you have let me alone?"

Her head lolled to the side, and she felt herself swaying, ready to give in to the moment, to let her body have its way. But...

He found her buttons and he finished undoing her blouse. The feel of him on her flesh made her moan. "Oh, please." She sighed, hating the slip of silk that was the last barrier. He unclasped her bra, brushed her rigid nipples with his palms, then cupped her in his hands.

She leaned in, reveling in the familiar touch, wondering how she'd gone so long without it. Not thinking about his words, only reacting to his touch.

His lips replaced his right hand. Licking, swirling, sucking her. His low growl was an animal sound. She arched her back, hanging on to his arms with clutching fingers. Then he reached down, and the sound of her zipper brought her out of her trance like a bucket of cold water. She stepped back, breaking his invisible hold on her. The air on her breasts made her feel incredibly naked, and she quickly covered herself with her blouse. "Stop," she said.

"Maggie, no."

She pushed past him, grabbed onto the closet door and forced it open. The light made her wince, and the thought of what she'd almost done made her cringe.

Turning to him, she saw the need and the hurt on his face, so plain and so raw that it made her chest squeeze tight. Then the look was gone, as abruptly as if he'd turned off a switch. Making her doubt. Making her unsure.

"Get out, Spencer."

"How can you say that after what we just did?" he said, his voice cool velvet. "After what we felt?"

She turned away, desperate to leave the closet and his proximity. "I'm not yours anymore," she said.

He came up behind her and took hold of her shoulders. "Yes, you are. You might marry another man, but you're mine. You'll always be mine. You can fool other people, Maggie, but you can't fool me. I know you too well. I know how your body aches, how it needs. I know every little quirk, every secret desire. And I know how to satisfy you, Maggie. Remember? Remember the nights on the living-room floor? How it felt when I made you come and come until you begged to have me inside you?" He moved his head down closer, so his mouth touched her ear. "Remember how you begged for it, Maggie?" he whispered. "How you screamed? I do. I remember it all."

"No," she said, twisting out of his grasp. "Don't do this to me. I stopped loving you. I stopped."

"Look at me," he said. "Look me in the eyes and say that."

She forced her gaze up, but she wasn't prepared for what she saw. His face was flushed, angry. As if she'd betrayed him by saying no. As if he had a right to her and was being denied.

"No," she said, shaking her head, not wanting any of it to be true.

"Yes. And in that closet last night, you remembered everything, too. You can't deny it. I felt you come. I felt how you wanted to scream again. Do you with Gary? Does he make you beg for it, too?"

"Stop it!" She turned away, ready to run, to hide. But he stopped her once more. His hand gripped her arm.

"Tell me what he's like, Maggie. Tell me what he does for you that I can't."

She whipped around to face him. "He's a gentleman," she said. "He would never do this."

"That's right. He wouldn't. He'd never strip you naked in a closet. He'd never push you against the wall and take you standing up. He's a gentleman. But you don't need a gentleman, Maggie. Because underneath those thousand-dollar dresses and those pearl earrings, you're no lady."

"That's where you're wrong," she said. "I've always been a lady. I just went slumming for a little while, that's all."

He jerked back, as if her words had punched him in the gut. She regretted saying them, wanted to take them back. He'd just confused her, made her angry.

He let her go. With his hand, at least. She could

feel him trembling now, using every muscle in his body to hold back his rage. He didn't stop staring into her eyes. Forcing her to face what she'd said and what her words had done to him. "It might have been slumming, but at least with me you were alive. You had dreams. You weren't a scared little ghost hiding behind your fancy address. At least, not until you destroyed it all. Or don't you remember that, either?"

He turned then and walked out the door. She stood still, trying to catch her breath. To calm her furiously beating heart. Now, more than ever before, she knew just how dangerous Spencer was. Because he knew who she really was.

7

SPENCER SLAMMED the door to the guest house. He
was furious with himself. He'd let his emotions
get the better of him, which was something he'd
trained himself not to do. He'd known being with
Maggie wasn't going to be easy, but the way she
made him feel was entirely unacceptable.

He went to the kitchen and poured himself a
glass of water. It was an effort to calm down, to
get himself under control. Thinking of what he'd
just done, how badly he craved her, shook him in
a way that threatened to undermine everything.

All he'd wanted was to convince her to go with
him when he looked at the house. He wanted to
see her eyes when she saw the kind of place he
could buy with a single phone call. To show her
what she'd given up. How the man she'd been so
ashamed of had turned out. And then he wanted
her to acquiesce. To come into his arms of her
own free will. To be his. But the plan had been for
him to feel nothing but satisfaction. Not to want
to keep her.

Now he wondered if he'd ever been in control.
Had his plan always included having Maggie forever? Winning her hand again? Had he just been
deluding himself?

That little scene upstairs had shown him that his need for revenge wasn't about money. At least not all of it. He wanted her to regret losing *him*. Not because he'd made it, but because she... Oh, dammit. Had he really come back here hoping she still loved him? Was it possible he still loved her?

He put down his water glass and went over to the club chair in the living room. He sat, but that was no good, so he got up again. He had too much energy, and he needed to do something. Work out, maybe, or climb Mount Everest.

Damn her! What kind of a hold did that woman still have over him? He should never have come back here. He was nothing but a fool.

There was no way he was going to take Maggie with him today. He didn't want her to see the house now. Maybe later, maybe when he figured things out. When he got his sanity back.

He got out his wallet, found the real estate woman's card, and called her. He postponed the appointment, telling her he'd call tomorrow.

Once he'd hung up the phone, he stood with his hand on the receiver. He thought about leaving, about checking into a hotel and saying the hell with it. But his business with Maggie wasn't finished. And if he wanted to get on with his life, that was something he'd have to do. Finish it between them. Once and for all. Let her go.

Or get her back.

No. He only wanted her now because he couldn't have her. He'd grown spoiled in the last year or two. When he'd wanted something, he'd gotten it. It wasn't that he still loved her. He just wanted to prove that he could have her.

He could imagine the reaction *that* would cause. Gary wouldn't be quite so glib after hearing his perfect wife-to-be wanted to go back to the mongrel she'd married before. And Betty would have to do some fancy backpedaling. She'd made it clear years before that he wasn't good enough for her daughter.

There was a certain satisfaction in knowing that he could turn their world upside down, but he'd also be putting Maggie through the wringer. Was it worth it? Just so he could win? Was that really who he was? What if he did get her back? Then what? Besides the passion, would there be enough there to make it with her for the long run?

Christ, he needed a drink. Or a psychiatrist. It had all seemed so simple. Come back to town, show Maggie, her family, the whole damn town, that despite all their certainty he'd never amount to anything, he'd made it and made it big. Then walk away. Simple, straightforward, satisfying. He'd just never considered that he would want her.

How could he have guessed that when she opened that closet door, she'd be opening Pandora's box? If he'd never touched her, never tasted her, none of this would be happening. But it was too late now. The feel of her had branded him, changed him from the inside out. He'd just destined himself to a lifetime of wanting something he shouldn't have.

Better to cut his losses now. Get the hell out of here. Now, before he did even more that he'd regret.

MAGGIE COULDN'T KEEP her hand steady. Her writing was crooked, as jagged as her nerves. She couldn't get Spencer's words out of her head. She struggled to concentrate on the seating chart. It had to be done by the end of the week, and at this rate, it wouldn't be finished for a month. She thought about throwing all the names into the air and letting the seats fall where they would. But she couldn't. The guests who were coming were a very mixed bag. Relatives—his and hers. Friends—his and hers and theirs. Business associates, prospective clients and, of course, the society mavens that could make or break them in the community. She needed all her faculties to do the job well. She'd be lucky if she could do the job at all.

She dropped her pen and sat back, amazed that the dining room looked so normal. How was it possible that so much had changed and yet remained the same? The china was back in the hutch, the candelabra were in their place on the sideboard. Mother had even brought out her Tiffany vase, which she'd stored for safekeeping. It all seemed unreal—the party, the orchestra, Spencer.

If only she hadn't mistaken him for Gary. If only she'd stopped the moment she'd kissed him. Why had he come back to torment her like this? Okay, so she was being punished. She'd been unthinking, more concerned with her image than with his pride. But this vengeance was too much. He had no right to twist up her life. She'd made peace with herself, reconciled to a life of calm but secure happiness. Not the kind of giddy, reckless bliss she'd had with her first marriage, but something strong and solid she could count on. Gary was a decent man. So what if she wasn't the center of his universe? He wasn't the center of hers.

Loving someone beyond reason was highly overrated. She remembered waiting for Spencer to come home, desperate if he was even five minutes late. Her world had been reduced to two very unequal states—Spencer and not Spencer. If he was there, she was happy. When he was gone, she felt as if a part of her heart was gone, too. The only time she was whole was when he was with her.

And she had thrived. She'd painted back then, and felt for the first time as though she had a right to her art. She'd dreamed more, too. She'd wanted to buy an art gallery. God, she hadn't thought about that in years. They'd planned it all together, down to the smallest details. He'd encouraged her dreams, pushed her to break free of her fears. And still she hadn't been satisfied. She'd wanted it all.

Spencer's unpredictability had excited her, and frightened her, too. She'd worried about introducing him to her friends, afraid they wouldn't understand him. Even after she saw for herself that he could fit in anywhere, she'd still worried that someone would discover his past, and...what? That she'd be shunned? Abandoned?

Fiona knew everything about Spencer, and she didn't care. So why had Maggie taken her mother's cautions so to heart? When she'd married Spencer, it had been against her mother's wishes, and Betty had made it vividly clear that she was making a terrible mistake. He'd drag her down. Embarrass her and her family. But he hadn't. Ever.

Now that he was back, he'd dredged up all the uncomfortable memories she'd finally managed to bury. Not just the wanting, but the insecurity. Spencer was danger, when all she longed for was safety.

Or did she?

She shivered with a sense memory so strong it nearly knocked the wind out of her. His hands on her naked flesh. Him pressing his body against her in the dark. The need for him consuming every other thought so that all she could do was whimper.

Damn him for coming back.

Maggie forced herself to pick up the pen. To look at the master list. To move Evelyn Craig from table twelve to eighteen so that she wouldn't have to sit with Donna Fairchild. She concentrated with everything in her, so when she heard the masculine cough, it made her jump and clutch at her chest.

"I'm sorry. I didn't mean to scare you."

She tried to calm down as she looked up at Spencer standing by the kitchen door. But her heart sped up, instead. "I thought you'd gone to look at houses."

He shook his head, loosening a small lock of dark hair so that it fell over his forehead. He pushed it back, and she felt the urge to touch his hair herself.

"What are you doing?" he asked. He pulled out the chair opposite her and sat down, staring at her papers.

"The seating plan," she said, willing herself to sound normal.

"How many people are coming to this thing?"

"Three hundred and twenty."

"Wow."

"Well, he's got a lot of friends, and there are his business associates..."

"That's a lot of presents though, huh?"

She nodded, grateful beyond measure that he wasn't going to bring up the business from before. That he was acting civilized and polite.

"Not like our wedding," he said, smiling. "Of course, no one knew we were going to run off and do such a crazy thing."

"Not even me," she said.

"It was a pretty good surprise, though, wasn't it? Maybe not fancy, but it was exciting."

She wondered why he was being so nice. No trace of this morning's anger showed in his face. The ferocity was gone so completely, it was as if it had never been there. But she couldn't get him to look at her. He just kept staring at the papers, at her hands.

"It was exciting," she said, grateful for the reprieve.

"What was that judge's name?" he asked, glancing at her quickly, then looking away again.

"Richard Rich," she said.

"Right, right. We thought our best man should be Scrooge McDuck, remember?"

She laughed. "And Huey, Dewey and Louie—"

"With Little Lulu as the maid of honor."

He grinned, the same infectious grin that had made her go out with him that first time. She hadn't wanted to, even though he'd looked like a younger, more handsome Clint Eastwood. But Fiona had twisted her arm. Then, when she'd opened the door that first night, he'd smiled at her, and she'd known everything would be okay. More than okay. And it was. That summer right after college, everything seemed possible. How incredibly long ago it all was.

"I'm sorry I didn't give you the kind of wedding you deserved."

She focused, unaware that she'd been staring at him. He wasn't grinning any longer. Instead, there was a look of regret on his face. Not harsh, not maudlin. Just a little sad. She shook her head, protective of those memories, the sweetest of her life. "It was perfect," she said. "I wouldn't have changed it for the world."

"But you didn't have your family there. Or your friends. Not even Fiona."

"I had you. That was all I needed."

"God, we were in love, weren't we?"

She nodded. "We were young."

"Yeah," he said, leaning forward and taking her hand. "And you were the most beautiful creature I'd ever seen. I knew I was the luckiest man on the face of the earth."

She felt his rough fingers brush her palm. Then, as if awakened from a dream, he sat back, pulling his hand away. He looked annoyed, as though he'd revealed more than he should have.

She looked away, embarrassed that she'd been lulled into letting her guard down. The early memories might be sweet, but they'd been usurped by words that could never be taken back. All the apologies in the world couldn't erase what she'd done to him. Or how he'd reacted.

He coughed, shifted in his chair. "Maggie," he said, his voice as soft as it had been before he'd pulled back.

"Yes?" She was wary this time. He could wound her so easily. And after this morning, she couldn't be more vulnerable.

"I'm sorry. I'm tense, that's all. Overtired, I suppose. I've been traveling a lot lately."

"Oh?" She looked at her lists as if she was actually reading them, but the words all blurred together.

"I'm moving my offices here."

"From where?" she asked, even though she knew. She knew a lot about Spencer. How he'd made a killing with his venture capital business after only two years as a broker. He'd been written about, lauded for his business acumen and marked as someone to watch by those in the know.

"Los Angeles."

"Funny," she said, daring a glance. "I would have figured you'd move to New York."

He shrugged. "L.A. won the coin toss."

"Lucky for you."

"Yeah. It was a good break. I had some luck as a broker. And then when I left... It all worked out."

"I'm glad."

Spencer smiled crookedly. "Are you?"

"Yes. I mean it. I'm glad for your success."

"You haven't done so badly yourself. Except..."

"Yes?"

He ran his fingers through his thick hair, and she knew he was debating whether to go on. When he looked at her, it was decisive. Whatever his doubts were, he'd tossed them aside.

"Maggie, what happened to the art gallery?"

"Oh," she said with a small pang of remorse. Right next to all the remorse she'd already been hit with in the past twenty-four hours. "It didn't happen," she said.

"Why not?"

She didn't want to talk about it with him. Not him. He'd been the keeper of her dreams for so long, she didn't want him to know that none of them had come true. "I got other interests," she said. "The shelters really eat up my time."

"Yeah," he said. "I can see where they would.

Last night was really something. A quarter of a million dollars is quite a haul."

She smiled. This was something she could be proud of. "In the past four years, we've raised almost two million. We have full-time counselors at every one of the shelters, and we do job training and parenting. We have child-care centers so the women can go out and find work. It's been so exciting to see it all happen."

"I have to admit, I was a little surprised."

"About what?"

"That you'd become so active in a charity like that."

"Why?"

He looked at his hands for a second before returning her gaze.

"Ah," she said, seeing the light flush on his cheeks. "You mean because I was so selfish."

"No, no. It's just that…"

"It's okay. I admit it. I was. I was a spoiled girl, and it took me a while to grow up. But I did grow up, Spencer. I'm not the girl you married."

"No, you aren't, are you?"

She couldn't tell if he was serious or mocking her. She used to know. She used to be able to read him like a book. But he'd learned how to use masks, at least for the most part. Back up in her room, in her closet, when she'd turned on the light, he hadn't been able to disguise his feelings then. He still hurt. Badly. And he still wanted her, just as she still felt his pull. But it was too late. Too much had occurred. They'd both made choices—one of which for her was letting go of her dreams of owning the gallery. She might regret having lost a dream, but she'd never regret what she'd chosen instead.

"I'm sorry," she said, "but I really have to get this done. Tomorrow I've got a million things to do. It takes a lot to put on a wedding these days."

He nodded, letting out a soft stream of pent-up air. She wondered if he was relieved about the change of subject. If he needed time to think, just as much as she did.

"I know you're busy tomorrow, but it would mean a lot if you'd come look at a house with me. Will you?"

"What time?" she said. Time alone with him, out of the house, away from her family and phones and seating charts, would give her the opportunity to finally get her apology out of the way. And by leaving it until tomorrow, she could sort out some of her jumbled thoughts.

"Whatever time you say."

"How about around noon? We can have lunch, and I should still be able to get everything done."

Spencer stood up. "Great." He looked into the living room, then toward the back of the house. "Everyone's gone, eh?"

"Mother's at bridge club and Caroline is at the mall. What's the matter? Nothing to do?"

"No, I have things to do. I'm going to go check on the new building. Make sure we're on schedule." He hesitated, then smiled. "Am I welcome at dinner?"

"As long as you behave yourself."

His laughter rippled through her, and the

sound was so familiar she felt that he was filling up an empty space in her soul she hadn't known was there. Spencer used to laugh a lot. So did she. What happened?

"I'll never behave myself with you, Maggie. Don't you know that by now?"

She did. She knew he'd never behave, and that his words would always have the power to hurt her, and that his touch would forever make her tremble. Despite her choices, despite trying her best to love Gary, Spencer still had her in the palm of his hand. Now, the tough part was going to be accepting that, and watching him walk away again.

8

THE KNOCK on her bedroom door awakened Maggie with a start. She'd been dreaming, troubled dreams, where she was yelling and yelling and no one would answer her. It took her a moment to realize she was safe, in bed, and that it was six at night, not six in the morning.

"Maggie? Are you all right?"

"Come in, Mom," she said, not willing to get up just yet. Her nap had made her feel groggy instead of refreshed.

The door opened and Betty, in her pale yellow slacks and blouse, complete with a perky little bumblebee brooch, walked in, shaking her head. "It's dinnertime, and here you are sleeping. There's so much to do in the next few weeks, Margaret. Did you get any of the seating plan done?"

"I did some," Maggie said. "But I think we need to sit down tomorrow and look at it together. I don't know a lot of the people you've invited, so I don't know where to put them."

That brought a smile to Betty's lips. "Of course I'll help you. It's not an easy job. So many personalities to contend with."

"I'd better get washed up for dinner," Maggie said, tossing her comforter aside.

"Can we sit for a moment first?" Betty asked.

Maggie nodded as her mother sat on the edge of the bed.

"It's about Spencer."

Maggie had already guessed that. What she didn't know was how angry her mother really was.

"I don't know what came over your father last night. He should never have agreed to have that man in our home."

"Daddy was thinking of me, that's all."

"What does that mean?"

Maggie sighed. Even though her mother knew about the falsified résumé, she'd never seen it as a problem. She thought Spencer was insane for not taking advantage of Maggie's kindness. "He knows I owe Spencer an apology."

"You most certainly do not. It's just the other way around, for heaven's sake. He walked out on you! After all you'd done for him. I still can't believe you don't see that. He should have been kissing your feet instead of stomping out like he was some wounded bear."

"Mother, I don't want to discuss this." Maggie stood and went to the dresser to get fresh clothes. She was still wearing her outfit from this afternoon, and only then did she realize she should have changed before taking her nap. But she wasn't thinking too clearly after her conversation with Spencer.

"It has to be discussed, Maggie. Your hoodlum ex-husband is living here while your fiancé is out of town. Just how do you think that looks? If you don't care for your reputation, at least have the decency to care about mine."

"He's in the guest house. There's nothing wrong with that."

"What are you saying? There are a million things wrong with that, starting with the fact that people are already talking about you two. Don't think our friends don't remember. They do. They know what kind of trash he comes from. They all know his mother was a prostitute and his father is a drunkard."

Maggie turned to face her mother, old anger and frustration bubbling inside her at this oft-repeated argument. "You don't know that about his mother. Even if you did, it doesn't matter. It never did. Spencer is his own man now. He's wealthy and successful. If people can't see that, then they're blind."

Betty stood. Her perfect hair, done each week by the most expensive stylist in Houston, quivered with her anger. Her normally pale complexion flushed with heat. "Margaret, I won't be disgraced again. I almost didn't survive the first fiasco, and I've never been more grateful to anyone than I was to Spencer Daniels when he walked out the door. Gary is a fine man, with a wonderful family and good breeding. You're just lucky he'd have you, after you'd been with Spencer."

"Stop it, Mother! Now. I won't do this. I'm not ashamed of marrying Spencer, do you hear me? I'm only ashamed of how I treated him afterward, when I thought he wasn't good enough. I was wrong. I shamed myself, don't you see?"

"I don't understand you at all," her mother said, walking to the door. "I thought I'd raised you better than this."

"You did. You raised me to have respect for other people, regardless of their backgrounds. Spencer never deserved less."

"He was trash. He still is trash, no matter how much money he's put into his bank account. You can't fix flawed furniture with a coat of paint, Margaret. No matter how you much you try to pass it off for something fine, the poor workmanship will always shine through."

"Please stop," Maggie said, holding on to her temper with all her fortitude. "I'm begging you. I won't ever agree with you about this. Ever."

Betty sniffed. "I just pray that Spencer's past doesn't come back to slap you in the face. Now, please get ready for dinner. Despite my wishes, we have a guest."

The door shut softly. Maggie stood still, holding a pair of lacy underwear in her hand. She couldn't believe her mother had so much stored vitriol, that she hated Spencer so much. They'd had similar conversations before, but she'd never exploded like that. Never said such hurtful things.

Betty had always treated Spencer cordially. Not warmly, and not like a son, but she'd been polite, and on occasion even sweet. And all the time, she'd felt that he was no better than dirt under her feet.

Maggie felt ashamed, but not just of her mother. Of the things she'd inherited from her mother. Maggie's faults were even more glaring, as they were couched in words of equality and fairness. Yet she hadn't been fair with Spencer, had she?

The first time she'd gone to his apartment—their apartment—she'd been horrified at how tiny and dingy it was. Hadn't she realized what her casual disdain had done to him? How small it made him? And yet all he'd done was kill himself working two jobs so that he could buy her a new couch, a new lamp. All he'd cared about was making her happy. Treating her like a princess, a goddess. And she'd let him know at every turn that it wasn't enough.

She'd returned the couch and bought a new one, one Spencer could never have afforded.

She'd bought him a whole new wardrobe, claiming it was to celebrate their new beginning, but in reality it was so she wouldn't be embarrassed to be seen with him.

Her father was right. She had taken away his pride, but not only with the résumé. It had begun long before that. What she couldn't imagine was how Spencer could have ever forgiven her, how he could even look at her.

She closed her open drawer and walked slowly to the closet. She didn't want to face him. She didn't want to sit at the table, knowing how her mother felt, knowing all she herself had done. But she would. She'd act as if nothing had happened. As if he was the most welcome of guests. Dammit, there had to be something about her "good breeding" that was worthwhile.

SPENCER THREW his towel on a chaise longue and studied the quiet calm of the well-lit swimming pool. It had been a very odd dinner, and he'd begged off early, intent on getting the exercise his body demanded of him. Normally, he ran. He also got into the gym a few times a week to do strength training, but he liked the running. He'd lived in the Hollywood Hills, and frequented an excellent track by a reservoir. He always went very early in the morning, before his hectic day began. Using the time to plan his schedule, he'd gone to work refreshed and able to face whatever came his way.

But it wasn't easy for him to run in Houston. Five years away had made him susceptible to the humidity. It would take a while to acclimatize again to this soggy weather.

So the pool had beckoned all evening, all during the strangely clipped yet oddly animated discussion at the dinner table. Betty had barely glanced at him, while Maggie had been almost too solicitous. Only Frank and Caroline had been their normal selves, and he suspected the two of them had caught wind that something was going on, too. He wondered if they understood that the problem centered around him. It was never said, but it was true nonetheless. His presence in this home was causing grief in every direction.

He took a great lungful of air and dived into the water. It was cool, but not cold. Almost not cool enough. Although he knew the pool wasn't heated, the hot summer air had been a natural heater.

But the water felt good on his body, and good for his mind. Swimming was something he'd learned late in life. High school. When most kids took swimming for granted. But he'd never been near a pool before that. When he was forced into learning to swim, it had turned into a lesson in humiliation. He'd been taunted unmercifully by the same wonderful kids who'd also made it a point to make fun of his clothes, his awful shoes, his meager lunches—when he had one. The worst of it, though, was when he'd fallen asleep in class. Most of the time, it was because his father had brought home his drinking buddies, and Spencer had been kept up all night with the noise in the small one-bedroom apartment. His bed was in the living room, and his father didn't let him use the bedroom, even when there was company. So he stayed up.

Spencer shut the unpleasant memory out, grateful that he hadn't been turned off swimming for good. Now he started his laps, working his muscles hard, up and down the length of the pool, back and forth, until he could feel himself growing weary. And then he pressed harder. Another lap, and another. Stretching himself, forcing his boundaries back. Finally, when it was beyond him to lift his arm even one more time, he stopped.

Turning onto his back, he closed his eyes and floated, breathing in great gasps of air until his lungs no longer complained. Then he could concentrate on the floating. On the feeling of weightlessness and freedom, the great stillness marred only by the sound of crickets out looking for a mate.

He felt her in the water before he heard her. A ripple that disturbed the calm. It was Maggie. He knew it. None of the other Beaumonts would come out here tonight. Caroline had a date, and Betty and Frank mostly forgot that they had a backyard.

He drifted, waiting to see if she would come to him. He thought of her in her bathing suit, but the image changed a second later to Maggie without her bathing suit. He'd never made love to her in a pool. In a shower, yes, but not a pool. He wondered about the logistics. If it was possible to keep lubricated while submerged. It was a foolish train of thought, and he had to turn over so she wouldn't notice his swimsuit tenting in the moonlight.

He dived under and saw her legs in the wavering light. A moment later he was next to her, flinging the water out of his eyes with a shake of his head.

"I didn't want to disturb you," she said, "but the water looked so wonderful. I don't know why I don't swim in the evening more. It's my favorite time."

"It's nice," he said, trying to gauge her mood. Her voice was normal again, not that higher, overexcited pitch from dinner.

She looked up and turned her head until she

found the moon. He'd noticed it earlier. Big and white and so clear he could almost see the American flag in the Sea of Tranquillity.

When he looked down again, she was smiling at him. "What?"

"I don't know. Something about the full moon, I guess. I was just wondering what time it was, and if you'd be turning into a werewolf soon."

He bared his teeth and growled for her, then listened to her laugh. That incredible sound. The moon did him a favor, and illuminated her face. He watched the way her eyes crinkled, how her teeth looked so very white, how the water droplets clung so prettily to the edge of her cheek.

He touched her arm, ran his hand from under her shoulder down to her hand, watching the trail his fingers had left on her skin.

"Spencer?"

"Hmm?"

"I'm sorry about dinner."

"Why are you sorry? I like chicken and mushrooms."

She pushed him lightly on the chest, making him lose his footing for a second, and when he settled back down he was closer to her. Almost touching.

"I didn't mean the food. I meant…Mother and I had a fight."

"Uh-huh. About me, I presume?"

Maggie nodded. "She doesn't think it's very appropriate for you to be here, especially when Gary's out of town."

"What do you think?"

She studied him for a long moment, then let her hand drift into his. "I don't know what to think. I'm not sure I understand why you're here."

"You're not?"

She shook her head.

"I'm here because of you." He moved those last inches until his bare chest touched the tips of her breasts. He wanted to strip off the small triangles of material that kept him from feeling her completely, but instead he ran his hand over her shoulders again, pushing her gently toward a more steady foothold.

She didn't fight him. She balanced herself by holding his sides, and as she touched him, he felt the reaction he'd tried to hide from her before come back full force. But he didn't hide it any longer. He rubbed against her, letting her feel the power she had over him.

Once he was sure he could stand and that she wouldn't slip away, he bent to her lips, kissing her gently while moving his hands around her back. He wondered if she'd pull away or if the moon had stolen her senses, too.

He had his answer when she took his gentle kiss and turned it into something deeper. He felt her tongue slip between his teeth, dip into his mouth to taste and to tease. He groaned as he teased her back, moved against her body, danced a dance they both knew by heart.

When he moved his hand to her bathing-suit top and slipped his fingers underneath the material, he teased her there, too. Just his finger on her puckered nipple, swirling the skin, jealous of the water for the places it could go that he could not.

Her hand came down on his and held it still. She broke the kiss with a sigh. "No, Spencer. Stop."

Stop? Stop when he had heaven in his arms? How could he?

He reached for her mouth with his lips, but she turned her head, stepping back out of his arms.

"We can't."

"You want it. I know you do."

"Yes," she said so softly the night breeze nearly carried the sound away. "But it's not right. I can't do this. Not to Gary, and not to myself. I can't be with you, Spencer, and you know it. This—" she moved her hand over her breast and down her stomach in an innocent gesture that had him aching "—this is something that's real, and it's powerful, but it's not enough. We know that, right? If it were, we'd still be together."

He wasn't strong enough to look at her and keep his distance. Instead, he slipped under the water, and used his arms to push himself to the other end of the pool. When he finally came up for air, he turned. She was where he'd left her. Beautiful in the moonlight. This was a little better, but not much. At least from here he couldn't look into her eyes and see the want she was denying.

"I meant to tell you when I came out," she said, her voice carrying neatly over the expanse of water. "I asked Fiona to come for a swim."

"Now?"

"Yes," she said. "I heard her car a minute ago."

"Safety in numbers, eh?"

She nodded. "It's best that we're not alone, Spencer. I don't want to do something I'll regret."

He wanted to tell her to not get married. That's what she'd regret.

"Yoo-hoo!" Fiona's voice interrupted his thoughts with a jolt. "Oh, swimming people! I've come and I've brought booze. Oh, and I've brought Josh, too." Her laughter bounced all over the patio.

Spencer was in no mood for laughter. The booze appealed though. He'd have a drink, maybe more. Enough to let him fall asleep without thinking.

He heard the sound of her dive only a second before her wake hit him. Another followed, this one bigger, as her boyfriend-du-jour jumped in after her. Spencer wiped his face, then started his swim to the shallow end of the pool.

Someone grabbed his leg halfway there. He broke free, and turned on Fiona. Her long hair was a wet mop of a bun on top of her head. She smiled at him. "Hi there, big guy."

It was probably a trick of the moonlight, but he could swear Fiona's smile was forced. That she was actually on the verge of tears, despite her cheery voice.

"What's wrong?" he asked.

She stared at him. Treading water, blinking. "How did you...?"

"Tell me, Fiona," he said. In back of him, he heard Josh introduce himself to Maggie.

"It's nothing," Fiona said, her voice much softer, much sadder.

"Did he do something?"

"Josh? No. He's a puppy dog. Just another puppy dog in my long line of puppy dogs."

"Have you been drinking?"

She laughed. "Oh my, yes. But I'm still not drunk. Why is that, Spencer? Why can't I get drunk tonight?"

He swam to her and took her gently around the shoulder, angling her so he could swim them both to the side of the pool. Once he got there, he made sure she was stable and that she wouldn't drown.

"Talk to me," he said.

She sniffed loudly. "There's nothing to talk about."

"It's Gary, isn't it?"

She stilled and her chin dipped beneath the water. "What?"

From the shock on her face, he knew he'd guessed correctly. He'd seen the way Fiona had looked at Gary last night. The longing he saw in her eyes was too much like what he saw in his own mirror for him to mistake it. "Does he know? Does Maggie?"

"No," Fiona said. "And I'll never tell them. You won't either, will you? Promise. Promise me, Spencer."

"All right. I won't say anything. But Fiona, what happened? How did you—"

"Get into this mess?" She smiled again, and if anything, it made him feel for her more. "I could ask you the same thing, couldn't I? Because no matter what you say, I know you're in love with Maggie. You always have been and, honey, I hate to tell you this, but you always will be."

"Are you two all right?"

Spencer turned at Maggie's voice. She sounded concerned, and if he didn't stop her, she'd be over here in a minute. He didn't want to do that to Fiona. "We're fine. Just plotting revenge."

"On whom?"

"All those lousy kids from high school," he said, hoping he sounded as if he was kidding around, that nothing was amiss. "You know. Scott Barnes."

"Jimmy Fallon," Fiona shouted.

"Tug Patterson," Spencer added, laughing. But he put his hand on Fiona's shoulder and squeezed it, letting her know that not only was her secret safe with him, but he knew his secret was safe with her.

9

MAGGIE GREW more and more curious. The day had begun with no sign of Spencer. His place at the breakfast table was set, but he wasn't there. Her family had gone to church, and she had lingered over coffee, wondering whether she should call the guest house or leave it alone.

Leaving it alone was, of course, the most prudent thing to do. She still felt guilty about yesterday. Twice, she'd let him kiss her. Twice, she'd kissed him back. She'd reveled in her indiscretion once she was in bed, not allowing thoughts of Gary or her duty to him to intrude. This morning, however, all she could think of was her betrayal. It was nothing less. She had no business kissing any other man, and most especially not Spencer. Not when he could turn her into jelly with a touch.

She'd done something before coming down to breakfast that she hadn't done in a very long time. She'd written in her journal. Put everything down on paper—her doubts, her fears, her feelings for Gary and Spencer. But instead of making things clearer, all the exercise had done was confuse her more.

In almost every way, Gary was the right man

for her. He was everything she was raised to want. Intelligent, financially secure, well placed socially, with a good family. And she knew he would make a good, if often absent, father to her children.

Spencer, on the other hand, had already proven to be inappropriate. Completely disregarding his unfortunate parentage, he was brash, arrogant in some ways, yet insecure in others, leaving him moody, hard to read, unpredictable. Instead of the placid journey that she could look forward to with Gary, Spencer offered a roller-coaster ride of heady highs and desperate lows. He was everything she'd vowed to avoid.

And yet, when he kissed her, all her logic and reason went out the window. Kissing Gary was like kissing a friend. Kissing Spencer was like... fireworks.

But making love was only a part of marriage. She knew from experience that it wasn't enough to make things last. It was the ordinary day-to-day that really made a marriage. Mutual respect, open communication, support, laughter.

She knew she had those things with Gary, at least to some degree. They talked easily, he respected her, and if he wasn't too overwhelmed with work, he had an easy, affable sense of humor. The support issue was a little murky. He'd never quite understood why she wasn't content to do the fundraising for the shelters. Why she insisted on counselling and even some rescue work. But in time, she was sure he'd come to see how important it was to her.

With Spencer, all those issues, except laughter, of course, were shaded in gray. She didn't know if he respected her. In fact, she doubted it, after what she'd done. Communication? They always seemed to fight, or to end up in each other's arms. Yesterday's talk at the dining-room table had been something of a surprise. She'd liked it, but she hadn't been completely at ease. Support? He'd always believed in her, but it wasn't the kind of support she was talking about.

From the moment they'd met, Spencer had put her on a pedestal. His image of her was idealized, and while that was flattering, it was also impossible to live up to. That had changed, of course, in the end, when she'd fallen so hard from that perch. But could time and distance have made him see her for who she really was? The bottom line was that until they cleaned up the past, she wouldn't know what they had. And she wouldn't know what to do.

So that was her mission. To take the opportunity of being alone with him today to finally apologize. To tell him all the things she should have told him years before. To wipe the slate clean, if he'd let her.

But maybe he'd changed his mind about taking her house hunting. It was almost eleven, and he still hadn't come in.

It was Cora's day off, so she took her plates to the kitchen. As she rinsed her cup, she looked out the window past the pool to the guest house. With the drapes drawn, she couldn't tell if he was up or not. Then her gaze went to the pool, and she thought about Fiona.

Something had been wrong with her last night, but Maggie wasn't sure what. It could have been that she was just dissatisfied with Josh, who was very sweet and very good-looking, but also very young. And, she had to admit, he didn't seem terribly bright. She wished Fiona could find someone. Someone she deserved, who would love her and appreciate her for all the incredible, albeit difficult, things she was.

Fiona had had too much to drink, which had become more of an issue of late. But Maggie was convinced that was a symptom, not a cause. What really worried her was that there seemed to be something strained between them. That had never happened in all the years they'd known each other. The tension had begun when Maggie had gotten engaged. She suspected that despite her words to the contrary, Fiona didn't like Gary, but that she was too good a friend to say anything. Perhaps, if they all spent a little more time together, Fiona would see that Gary was a nice guy.

When he got back to town, Maggie would see to it that Gary and Fiona had more of a chance to know each other. She didn't want anything to come between Fiona and herself. Fiona was her touchstone.

Something caught her attention, and she looked at the guest house again. There he was. Spencer closed the door behind him and started toward the house. Maggie's pulse quickened and she felt that weird little shimmy in her stomach that was part anticipation and part fear.

How could he still do that to her? After all they'd been through? It wasn't fair, not to her. Not to Gary. Today, it was apologize or die trying.

SPENCER HADN'T TOLD HER anything, just that the house was in River Oaks, not too far from her parents' place. He'd been mysterious and quiet, which made her even more nervous about what she had to do. She wondered if he, too, had been thinking about yesterday, about what they'd said to each other. She wanted to ask him what he wanted. Sex? That wouldn't happen, despite her inability to say no to his kisses. But she wouldn't make love to him again, not while she was engaged to Gary. Did he want her back? That seemed impossible. No, he probably wanted what she did—to make things right between them so he could get on with the rest of his life. If he was buying a house, it must mean that he planned to fill it with a wife and kids. Otherwise, he could have gotten an apartment or condo.

She studied him as they drove in silence, turning from one tree-lined street to another. The homes here, all of them, were in the million and up range. Big brick structures with manicured lawns and huge front windows. It was the wealthiest section of Houston, a place he'd never seen until he'd started dating her.

"Here it is," Spencer said as he turned into a circular driveway.

Before her was a mansion, not a house. Bigger by half than her parents palatial home. Huge, ancient magnolia trees stood guard in front of the white columns. The house itself was Late Georgian. The architecture made it a showplace.

He pulled his car behind a beige Mercedes. Before Maggie had a chance to say a word, he hopped out, came around to her side of the car and opened the door.

"This is some house," she said, amazed at the architectural details in the windowsills and corners.

"It has possibilities," he said.

He led her up the stairs to the front door, which opened before he knocked. A very pretty woman with long, flowing hair, wearing a very tight red suit and killer stilettos waved them in.

"Welcome, Mr. Daniels," she said, her voice all honey and Southern charm. "And you must be Mrs. Daniels."

Maggie felt a jolt inside her at the use of her former name. It had been so long since she'd called herself Mrs. "This is Ms. Beaumont," he said.

"Oh," the young woman said. "I'm sorry. I thought you said…"

"Yes, well… Maggie, this is Ms. Nickson."

"Call me Susie, please," she said, holding out a manicured hand. "Let me show you around."

Maggie shook her hand and forced a smile as she wondered what Spencer had told the woman, or if Susie had just misunderstood.

"First, let's take a look at the living room, shall we?" Susie said, walking briskly across the Italian tiles of the foyer. Spencer gestured with his hand for Maggie to go first, but she didn't move off right away. Instead, she whispered, "Mrs. Daniels?"

"It was a miscommunication," he said. "A mistake."

"I see," she said, but she still wondered.

She set off after the real estate agent, with Spencer close by. Close enough that if he reached out, he could touch her.

For the next hour, the twenty-something woman gave them a dazzling monologue on the benefits and bonuses of buying the mansion.

Spencer hardly paid attention to Susie, however. He kept looking at Maggie, watching her with a peculiar mix of anticipation and disappointment. As if he'd expected something from her that she wasn't delivering, even though she was quite vocal in her admiration of the house.

How could she not be when she saw the incredible gourmet kitchen, the indoor Olympic swimming pool, bathrooms larger than most hotel rooms. And a little something special that made Maggie's breath catch—a library right out of the old English movies she'd loved her whole life, complete with movable ladder, fireplace, wing chairs and even a stunning handmade lap blanket on the couch.

"I thought of you when I heard about this room," Spencer said. "You told me once you wanted a library that would make Henry Higgins green with envy."

Hearing those words—the exact words she'd

said to him one night, she couldn't remember the date, while passing a bookstore on their way to a movie—stunned her. She'd never expected him to remember something like that. And why would the fact that he did make her feel like crying?

Susie and Spencer had moved ahead while she'd lingered in the library. Maggie turned to see them halfway up the stairs, Susie in the lead, making sure her tightly encased derriere wiggled enticingly. Maggie hurried to catch up. The master suite was up there, and given the grandeur of the rest of the house, she couldn't even imagine what was in store.

Whatever she'd imagined, it hadn't been close. This wasn't a master bedroom. This was a palace. The California king-size four-poster bed didn't even look big. Not even the platform helped. The carpet was so thick she thought she'd lose her shoes in it. They could have cooked half a cow in the fireplace and still would have had room to roast the marshmallows. The corner group, a couch, two chairs, coffee table, would have looked wonderful in a large living room. Then there was the armoire, so gorgeous it had to have been built specifically for this room by an expert craftsman.

"I knew you'd love it," Susie said, moving very close to Spencer. She took him by the hand and walked over to the bed. With her free hand she smoothed down the already pristine bedspread, all the while looking at him with her big, hungry eyes.

Maggie had been picking up on her flirting all along, but this was the first moment she'd seen the real estate woman be so overt. Although she understood that Susie knew she and Spencer weren't married, they hadn't made their relationship clear, and frankly, Susie was ticking her off.

"Spencer," Maggie said, keeping her tone light, "come look at this."

He turned toward her and she had to think fast. There was a rather ugly statue of a nude woman on a pedestal, and she pointed to it as if it were the *Venus de Milo*.

Spencer, looking a little puzzled, left Susie's side and came next to Maggie. "That's…nice."

"It is, isn't it, hon?" Then she took his hand in hers and led him toward the master bath.

"What's this?" he asked.

"A bathroom."

"No, I meant *this*," he said, holding up their entwined hands.

She let him go immediately. "Oh, for heaven's sake. It was a way to get you to come with me. That's all."

He smiled. "How do you like Susie?"

"Shh. She'll hear you."

He turned and shut the bathroom door. "So?"

Maggie suddenly found the bidet utterly fascinating. "She's very nice. Although…"

"Yes?" he said, moving right next to her.

"Nothing. She's great. She's the queen of real estate ladies."

"You're jealous."

"Don't be ridiculous. Isn't it time for lunch?"

He laughed, the sound echoing off the tile walls of the huge room. "And here I was thinking you didn't care."

"I don't. Not in that way."

"Ah, Maggie, your lips say you don't, but your eyes…"

"My eyes haven't spoken in a really long time, Spencer. Are you going to buy the house or not?"

"What do you think I should do?"

She looked around, really seeing the bathroom. It was fabulous. The Jacuzzi tub was large enough for a party of four. The shower had several showerheads, and was a work of art in itself. There were two sinks, plenty of storage space, and the tiles and wallpaper were stunning in their cool blue-and-white simplicity. "It's a great house."

"Somewhere you'd be happy? Theoretically speaking, of course."

"It's a little on the large side."

"But not if you had, say, three or four kids."

"Theoretically," she said.

He nodded.

Three or four kids. That had been the original plan. One thing she'd always known was that Spencer would make a terrific father. He'd give his kids everything, all he'd never had as a child. But the plan had fallen apart. Shattered. "I think you have to be the one to decide if you'd like it here. It's going to be your house, after all."

He walked over to the toilet and flushed it. The sound was so soft, Maggie figured it had to be some special, and expensive, design.

"So how come you still live with the folks?"

She jerked her attention from the toilet to Spencer. The question had come from nowhere. His gaze was still captured by the intricacies of indoor plumbing, but she knew he expected an answer.

"I moved in with them after we broke up. It was supposed to be temporary, but then I got involved with the shelters, and I never took the time to look for my own place."

He moved over to her, then touched her hair, taking a small strand between his thumb and finger. "What about you and Gary? Where are you two going to live after…"

"I'm going to move into his house after the wedding."

"Ah."

She watched his fingers, then moved her gaze to his eyes. He seemed strangely mesmerized by her hair, bewildered by the texture. "What?" she asked.

"I remember this," he said. "I've never felt anything like it. It's so soft, so beautiful."

"It's just hair."

"No. It's your hair." Then he moved his fingers to her cheek, touching her with the same reverence. "Your skin," he said, caressing her as gently as a breeze.

His gaze met hers and held her steady. Deep blue, inquisitive, imploring. He moved closer. She knew he was going to kiss her, that she'd decided this morning, once and for all, that she couldn't let that happen. Not again. It wasn't right. It wasn't…

His fingers played on her skin, and he looked at

her with such longing, she felt her resolve disappear right down the drain.

She closed her eyes as his lips brushed hers. "Your lips," he whispered, his breath warm and sweet. Then he kissed her. His mouth barely touched hers at first. Just a soft, tentative touch that lit a slow fire inside her. He toyed with her until she couldn't stand it any longer, and she moved that last inch.

She felt his arm go around her waist as he pulled her close. At the same time, he tasted her, brushing his tongue across her lips, teasing her into tasting him back.

"Yoo-hoo!"

Maggie broke away, stepping back so fast her legs hit the bidet, knocking her off balance. Just as Susie walked in, she sat down hard.

"Oh, I'm sorry," Susie said, her cheeks infusing with pink. She turned around quickly. "I didn't think…"

Maggie stood up, trying to stop her own blush. "It's all right," she said. "I wasn't…"

"There's only the closet and the guest bedroom left," Susie said.

Spencer looked at Maggie. "The closet?"

"No!" she said.

Susie looked confused. Spencer smiled at Maggie, then turned to the lady in red. "There's no need to look further. I've already made up my mind. I'll take it."

Susie lit up like a Christmas tree, no longer concerned about Maggie's indelicate position. "Really?"

"If we can work out the price."

"Oh, goodness. Yes, of course. If you'll follow me, we can start on the paperwork right away."

Spencer shook his head. "I've got to take Ms. Beaumont home. Why don't you put everything together, and I'll call you about setting up a time to talk."

"Oh, sure. Sure. I'll do that."

"Thank you," he said. "We can find our own way out."

"Oh, my. Okay, fine."

Maggie could fairly see the dollar signs dancing in Susie's eyes. The commission on this place would be enormous. Susie grinned broadly as she left the bathroom.

Spencer turned to Maggie. "Sure you don't want to see the closet?

She didn't answer. She had some questions of her own to ask. "Why are you taking this place?"

"Because I like it."

"Honestly?"

He nodded.

"It has nothing to do with me."

He shook his head. "No. It doesn't." He smiled enigmatically. "It did, but it doesn't now. Not in the same way." He looked around the huge bathroom, the sparkling tiles and glittering mirrors. "This is a place I can live the rest of my life. I can have a family here. A future."

A knot constricted her chest, completely surprising her with its intensity. The thought of him settling down with another woman, having children with someone else, made her reaction to Susie seem like a hiccup.

"What's the matter?" he asked, moving closer to her, touching her arm lightly with his hand.

She jumped back as if she'd been burned. "Nothing. Nothing at all. Congratulations on the house, Spencer." And then she turned toward the door, forcing herself not to run.

10

SPENCER PULLED his rented Mercedes into the parking space behind the wedding boutique and cut the engine. He didn't open the door immediately, even though the intense heat started to take over the interior before he'd even exhaled. Maggie didn't know he was picking her up. Fiona had called him a half hour ago, asking if he could do her this favor. He'd wondered if it was a ploy on Fiona's part, but she really had sounded stuffed up and miserable. On the other hand, Fiona was known for her acting ability.

He got out of the car and pocketed his keys. The two women had spent the evening together. He hadn't seen Maggie at all since he'd brought her home after showing her the house. She'd gone off to plan her wedding and he'd holed up.

The long night had given him ample opportunity to think about how his master plan had gone all to hell.

He'd been so sure about what he wanted. All of it tied up to the moment that Maggie got a load of the house he was going to buy, and all it represented. So why hadn't he felt victorious? Why hadn't her wide-eyed view of the outrageously expensive place given him one iota of satisfaction? Instead, all he'd felt was regret.

He couldn't even buy the house now. He didn't want it for himself, or for any future family he might have. Not after he'd seen Maggie's face at the sight of the library. Not after he'd seen her in the bedroom.

He'd tried to regroup. Come up with a new plan of attack. But the sad truth was, he didn't want revenge anymore. At 2:00 a.m. he'd finally given in and accepted that he wanted her back. That he'd always wanted her back.

But that wasn't going to happen. It couldn't. Not just because of Gary, not just because of all they'd been through, but because he still didn't deserve her. Not after making his fortune, not after becoming the man she'd said she wanted. What she didn't know, and what he could never tell her, was that it was all built on lies. His whole life was a house of cards that could be blown away, and he would never ask her to be part of that.

She had wanted him to be something he wasn't, and he'd walked out of her life because of it. And then he'd taken her lies and made them his own.

Up until yesterday, he'd convinced himself that it didn't matter. That his mistake was well in the past, and had no bearing on his life now. Yesterday had been a rude awakening. The past never goes away. It just lies in wait.

Now, though, it was Maggie who was waiting. He opened the door to the boutique, a little bell announcing his arrival. Maggie wasn't there, at least not that he could see.

An older woman in a blue dress walked from behind the counter. She looked him over from head to toe in one quick glance and evidently approved, if her smile was any indication. "May I help you?"

"I'm here to pick up Maggie Beaumont."

"Ah. I wish I could show you what an exquisite bride she is."

"I'd like to see that."

"But it would be bad luck."

He shook his head. "I'm not the groom."

The woman, who looked like the very model of a bride's mother with her pearl earrings and the little corsage on her dress, seemed shocked. "I thought..."

"Just a friend," he said.

"I see. Then I'm sure it would be fine for you to join her in the fitting room. Come with me."

Spencer followed the woman behind the pale curtain leading to the inner sanctum. A few more steps and he entered a large room with mirrors all around and a big round platform in the middle. Maggie stood on the pedestal, looking like an angel in white. It was as if she'd stepped out of his dreams, the way he'd always pictured her. Okay, not in a wedding dress. Frankly, not in any dress. But he'd always seen her in the center of his universe, surrounded by reflections of his feelings for her. "Wow," he said, simply unable to come up with anything better.

She saw him reflected in the mirror in front of

her. Her hands fluttered to her bodice as she spun around to face him. "What are you doing here?"

"Fiona asked me to come. She's not feeling well."

Maggie looked suspicious. "She was fine last night."

He shrugged. "She didn't sound fine when she called me. But then, you know Fiona better than I do."

Maggie pressed her lips together for a second. "Yes, I do."

"You're beautiful," Spencer said.

She looked down and straightened the bottom of the dress. "Thank you."

"He's a lucky man."

"I... Are you sure you don't have something better to do? I can always call a taxi to get home."

"No, no. I want to be right here."

Just then, a woman he hadn't seen before came from somewhere in the back. She was short, plump and had a weird sort of pincushion corsage on her wrist.

"Mrs. King, this is Spencer Daniels," Maggie said. "Mrs. King is the seamstress."

"How do you do?" Spencer said.

The woman looked up at Maggie with a puzzled frown. "I thought his name was Gary."

"Oh, I'm not marrying him. Spencer, I mean. We used to be married. But not anymore."

Mrs. King turned to Spencer. "You're her ex-husband?"

He nodded.

"Interesting," she said. Then she took Maggie's

right sleeve, pulled it down and started sticking pins in the fabric.

"He's just here visiting," Maggie said. "For the reunion. You remember, I told you about that?"

"Uh-huh," Mrs. King said, inserting pins at a dangerous clip.

Spencer walked over to the wall and leaned against it, staring at Maggie in her gown, forcing himself to smile. It was right that he was here. Penance for wanting to hurt her. Poetic justice that instead of making her beg to take him back, he had to will himself not to beg her. If penance was called for, then so be it. Maybe this kind of pain was what he needed to knock some sense into his head.

"So where are you two going on your honeymoon?" he asked, digging the knife in deeper.

"New York," she said.

"Niagara Falls?"

She shook her head. "Manhattan. We're staying at the Plaza. Going to the theater. That kind of thing."

"Nice."

"Yeah."

"Not like our honeymoon."

She didn't say anything at all. Mrs. King walked around to her other sleeve and busied herself pinning that. Maggie just stared at him, her gaze and his locked in mutual memories.

They'd gone all the way to Galveston after the wedding, about fifty miles. He'd booked them a room at a motel, nothing fancy. He hadn't had money for fancy. Three nights they'd stayed in their room, ordering meals and wine, half watching movies, entwined in tangled sheets. Those had been the best damn three nights of his life.

A beeper sounded, muffled but insistent, and Spencer automatically went for his pocket. Of course, it couldn't be his—he'd left his beeper in his suitcase.

"Oh, I think that's mine," Maggie said. "Spencer, could you look in my purse, please?"

He followed her gaze to find her pocketbook, and opened it. Thankfully, the beeper was on top. He always felt weird with women's purses, as if some scary feminine product was going to pop out and bite him. "It's you," he said.

"What's the number?"

He read it off, and she instantly looked worried. "Mrs. King," she said. "I'm sorry. I need to use the phone." Then she turned to Spencer. "The cellular is in there, too."

He moved her wallet and saw the little phone. After he gave it to her, he went back to his post by the wall.

Maggie dialed, and whoever she called must have answered on the first ring, because she said, "Hello," an instant later. Then she just listened, her expression growing more and more concerned.

"I'll be right there," she said. "Hold on a second, Pat." She looked at Spencer. "Can you write this down? I've got a notebook and a pen in my bag."

He obliged, her gravity making him hurry. Once he had the pen poised, he nodded.

"Sixteen twenty-seven Fondren. Apartment twenty-two. Okay, Pat. I've got it covered." Maggie hung up the phone. "I'm sorry, Mrs. King, but I have to go. Now."

Mrs. King didn't blink. She just went to Maggie's back and unzipped the gown.

Without pausing, Maggie let the dress fall from her shoulders. She was in a white petticoat. Nothing terribly risqué. He could see her bra straps, but nothing more. And yet the sight of her like that, undressing in front of him so casually that he might as well still be her husband, did something terrible to his gut. He turned away, focusing on putting her notebook back in her purse.

"I've got to go help someone move," Maggie said, stepping down from the platform. "This woman, she's in a bad situation. Her husband's gone, but she's not sure for how long. She needs me to get her and her daughter to the shelter."

"You? I thought all you did was—"

"No, I do more than raise money. I do whatever is needed."

He couldn't have been more surprised. But then Maggie had been nothing but surprises since he'd returned.

He hurried out, confused, still reeling from seeing her in that dress. Trying hard to accept that Maggie had grown up all on her own and he hadn't been around to watch.

THE APARTMENT was terrible. It was too warm, the old air conditioner sticking out of the second-story window loud with effort but losing the battle. The red carpet was black in spots, gray in others, the walls were a dingy tan that might have been white once upon a time. From where they stood just inside the front door, she could see the tiny kitchen, the living room and hallway. It was neat, but everything in it looked as if it had been broken at one time or another, and patched haphazardly with duct tape or glue.

Kristen Boyd, the woman who'd called for help, held her little girl's hand. They both looked terrified, and Maggie could see immediately that she had to get them out quickly. Kristen's right eye was swollen almost shut, her lower lip puffed out and red. The little girl looked okay, just scared to death.

"I'm Maggie," she said, speaking in a very low, calm, controlled voice. She needed to make sure Kristen trusted her, and that she knew Maggie was going to take her somewhere safe.

"This if my friend Spencer," she said, feeling him right behind her. "Are you packed?"

Kristen nodded, but she didn't move.

Maggie turned to the girl. "Where are your bags, honey?"

The little girl pointed toward the hall.

Spencer moved in front of Maggie, and Kristen took an automatic step back. Per Maggie's instructions, he stopped, then squatted so that he was eye level with the girl. "What's your name?" he asked, his voice just as soft as Maggie's had been.

"Tina," the little one said. She was pretty, but

her blond hair was a tangled mess, her jumper stained. She wore no shoes.

"Tell me, Tina," he said. "Do you have a favorite doll?"

She nodded, never letting go of her mother's hand.

"Why don't we go get your doll, and you can show me where the suitcases are. Okay?"

She looked up at her mother, who gave her a stilted nod.

Spencer held out his hand, and Tina cautiously took it. Then he stood and let Tina lead the way.

Once they'd gone into the hallway, Maggie moved closer to Kristen. "Are you hurt? I mean, is anything broken?"

Kristen sniffed, thought for a moment, then lifted her left hand. The pinkie finger stuck out at an odd angle, broken.

"Okay, we'll stop by the ER on the way to the shelter, okay?"

"He'll find us," she said, her voice as weary and battered as her body.

"No, he won't. We'll make sure. I promise you'll be safe. You have my word."

"That can't stop him."

"No one knows where the shelter is, Kristen. It's not listed in the phone book, and none of the hospitals even have the address. But we have to hurry."

Kristen jerked around as Spencer walked into the living room carrying two small suitcases. Tina had a naked Barbie tucked under her arm.

"Is this it?" Spencer asked.

Kristen nodded. Maggie opened the front door and waited for Kristen to take her giant step. It was terrifying living with a brutal man, but just as terrifying to walk out to an unknown world without money or a job or any confidence. It took Kristen a while, but when Tina grabbed her hand, the woman gathered whatever strength she had left and walked out of the only life she knew.

When Maggie looked at Spencer, she was surprised at his expression. He wasn't looking at Kristen or Tina. He stared at her oddly, as if he'd never seen her before. There was no time to ask him about it.

IT WAS PAST MIDNIGHT by the time Spencer drove into Maggie's driveway. He pulled to a stop and turned off the engine, then turned to look at her. She had fallen asleep, her head leaning against the cold window. He wanted to move her—but not wake her—so that she leaned her head on his shoulder.

The irony of the image wasn't lost on him. Today, he'd learned that Maggie didn't need anyone's shoulder to lean on. Not his, not Gary's. She'd told him she wasn't the girl he'd married, and now he understood how true that statement was. Maggie had turned into a woman. A capable, strong, independent woman. He'd been fooled because she still lived with her parents. He'd thought she'd gone there for safety, but now he didn't think so.

She'd taken care of Kristen and Tina all through the long afternoon at the emergency room, and then when they'd gotten to the shelter, Maggie had seen to it that they were fed, had beds to sleep in, that Tina understood that she could play with the toys in the play area. But it was what she'd done for Kristen that really struck him. By the time they left, the scared, almost catatonic woman who had answered the door at 1627 Fondren was smiling. Not a big smile, but a hopeful one. Which seemed to Spencer a small miracle.

All because of Maggie. The woman he'd sought vengeance against. The woman he'd wanted to see on her knees, crying that she'd lost everything when he'd walked out her door.

Talk about your wake-up calls.

As if she'd been listening in on his thoughts, Maggie sat up. She looked exhausted, but, oh, so beautiful. When he'd first met her, he'd been awed by her looks, by her bearing. She was a goddess, someone a mortal like him could never hope to touch. And yet she'd let him in.

It seemed that some things hadn't changed all that much. Although he knew her Achilles' heel, she was still a goddess, while he'd become much more mortal.

The thought came to him, so clear and sharp it almost hurt in its intensity. He hadn't left her because she'd lied on his résumé. He'd used the lie as an excuse to leave, because he knew he hadn't been, and could never be, good enough for Maggie. Despite her words, her kisses, her willing body, he'd never really believed she could love him.

Things really hadn't changed.

"What's wrong?"

Her voice startled him. He'd been so stung by his own admission that he'd forgotten she was there, that they were still in the car. "It's late," he said, hurrying out, afraid she'd seen too much.

"Spencer," she said, but he cut her off by closing his door. He walked around to her side and let her out, but his manner was brusque, discouraging conversation.

"What is it?" she said, ignoring his signals.

"I'm tired, that's all. And so are you. I'll see you in the morning." He started to walk away, but she stopped him with her hand on his shoulder.

"Come in with me?"

He didn't look at her. "I don't think that's such a good idea."

"Please?"

He couldn't refuse her. He took her hand and led her up the walk to the front door. She already had her key out, and she led him inside, the light on the second floor giving enough illumination so that he could make his way behind her. He could see how hard it was for her to climb the stairs. Each step was an effort. She'd be asleep the moment her head hit the pillow.

The door to her room was open, and after she stepped inside, she tossed her purse on the bed, then turned to Spencer. "Thank you for all you did tonight," she said.

"I didn't do anything. It was all you."

She smiled. "Let's just say we made a good team."

He reached out and touched her cheek with the

back of his hand, loving the feel of her, knowing he wouldn't be touching her again. "Maggie, I..."

She took his hand in hers and brought the palm to her lips, stealing his words and his determination. It was time for him to leave, not just her bedroom, but her life. He should never have come in the first place.

"I'm glad you were with me," she said, her voice roughened by the strain of the day. "I wanted you to see."

"I saw," he said. "What you've done is incredible, Maggie. You've helped so many people."

She studied his eyes, but he knew she couldn't see him. The light came in from behind him, so that he was in shadow. She wasn't though. He could see the tenderness in her eyes, and the sadness. "Why couldn't I help you?" she whispered. "Or myself?"

"You didn't do anything wrong," he said, wanting to kiss her. One last kiss, and then he'd leave.

"If I didn't do anything wrong, why did you go?"

God, the pain he'd caused her. Nothing but grief. Nothing but heartache. He steadied her with his hand, meaning to go, determined to walk away for good. But then she sighed, and he was helpless. He kissed her, crushing her lips with his, groaning under the weight of his own sorrow and the knowledge that no matter how bad he was for her, he still couldn't leave her be.

She ran her hand over his back, and as she reached his neck, the light in the room came on.

He looked up, startled as hell. His gaze jerked over to the lamp.

And Gary. Sitting on the chair by her bed.

11

Maggie's mouth opened, but she couldn't seem to form any words. Gary sat perfectly still on her blue velvet wing chair, as if he'd paid a ticket to watch a tragedy and was waiting for the last act. Only his eyes betrayed his personal interest in what was before him. His eyes that had always seemed so cautious were now filled with an anger she'd never seen before.

"What are you doing here?" she asked, surprised at how calm she sounded when her heart drummed so furiously in her chest.

"I came home early," he said, his voice like ice. "Surprise."

"Gary," she said, taking a step toward him. "It's not what you think."

"No? I'm a pretty observant fellow. I know what I saw."

"It was my fault," Spencer said.

Maggie turned her head at the sound of Spencer's voice. He seemed as calm as Gary. And just as cold.

"I was saying goodbye," Spencer said, his gaze locked on to her fiancé's. "I had no business kissing her, and I'm sorry about that. But you have nothing to worry about. I'm leaving. And I won't be back."

Maggie's chest constricted so tightly that she could barely breathe. She wanted to tell him no, that he couldn't go, but that was wrong. The man she loved was sitting in the chair. Not by her side. The man she was going to marry was the one she should be concerned about.

"Don't let me stop you," Gary said. "You'll forgive me if I let you see yourself out."

Spencer nodded, then slowly moved so that his gaze fell on Maggie. "I'm sorry," he said, but so softly she doubted the words carried to the chair behind him. "Goodbye, Maggie."

He turned to leave, and without even thinking about it, her hand went out to stop him. But Spencer didn't look back.

"Now's your chance," Gary said. "If you want him, go on, go after him."

She pulled her arm to her side and turned once more to face her future husband. "It's complicated," she said. "But it's not about us. That…had nothing to do with you."

"No?"

She shook her head, wanting to move closer to Gary but unable to make her feet move. "We had unfinished business," she said, knowing those feeble words couldn't possibly encompass all the heartache, pain and broken promises that had surfaced when Spencer had walked back into her life.

"Is it finished now?"

Gary's voice sounded so calm she might have

been fooled into thinking he didn't care. But the anger was still there. Controlled, yes, but simmering just below the boiling point.

"I think so," she said, wishing she could be definitive, wishing she still didn't want to rush out the door and find Spencer in the guest house. The division inside her was so sharp it was like a razor's edge. In front of her was the future she'd worked so hard for. The sanity she'd begged for. The man who could guarantee the kind of life she was supposed to have. Yet it felt as though her heart had just walked away.

"You think so," Gary repeated. He stood, and for the first time she noticed the similarity between the two men. They were both strong, with wide shoulders, slim hips. They both had those long legs, and carried themselves with great strength and dignity. But Maggie knew the difference. Gary's strength was solid, like a rock, while Spencer's was volatile, like a rocket engine on the launch pad, trembling with the force of its restrained power.

One so safe, one so dangerous.

"Let me tell you some things about your exhusband," Gary said, moving toward her slowly. She noticed his hands. Instead of the curled fists she'd anticipated, they were relaxed, polished, almost pretty. It seemed odd that his fury didn't reach his fingers.

"I've done a little checking on your boy," he said. "His empire isn't on very solid ground. He's made a big splash with a couple of good companies, but his track record is far from perfect. It could all go in a minute. One bad move, and he's back to square one."

"Gary, stop it," she said. "I don't want to hear this."

"But that's not the worst," he continued as if she'd never spoken. "There's something very fishy about his past, about how he got into Merrill Smith in the first place. I don't have all the facts yet, but when I do—"

"Gary, don't. I mean it. Don't do this. It's not necessary. Spencer and I are through. It's over and it has been for years. I admit, I got carried away, but it was all about the past, not the present. There's no reason for you to go digging into his life."

"I'll be the judge of that," he said, moving the last few steps between them. He was close enough now that he could touch her, but he didn't. His hands were still at his sides.

"I'm asking you to stop," she said, looking into his eyes, surprised by the intensity of what she saw there. Where had all that passion been hiding? Was it only when competition surfaced that Gary was able to get excited about her?

"I won't promise anything," he said. "Not after what I saw tonight."

"Gary, if you do this—"

"What?" His hands grabbed her arms, and he held her steady. "You'll call off the wedding?"

She didn't move, didn't dare blink. The pressure on her arms built, but she didn't respond. He'd seen her kiss Spencer. And she was terribly aware of the kisses Gary hadn't seen. She wouldn't stop him from hurting her.

"Do you still love him?"

She should say no. She should deny it with every breath in her body. "I don't know."

Gary let her go, but she took his hand in hers, forcing him to keep looking at her. "I do know that you and I are right for each other. What Spencer and I had was something different. Something that wasn't good for me. I know that. I don't want it again. Please believe me."

"So I'm supposed to be content with you still loving him, but marrying me?"

"I didn't say I loved him."

"But you didn't deny it."

"Gary, please. I'm so tired and so confused. Can't you please just trust me for a little while longer?"

He moved, breaking her hold on him. "I don't know."

"We'll talk again tomorrow. I promise. After we've both had some sleep."

He took in a great breath of air and let it out slowly, and she could almost see him willing himself to be calm. "All right. I'll be here tomorrow after work."

She sighed and closed her eyes. She didn't deserve it, but she'd won a reprieve.

"But he'd better be gone," Gary said as he walked to the door. "I don't want you to see him again. Ever." He watched her, his gaze burning her until she nodded. Only then did he leave.

She listened to his footsteps until they disappeared. Once he was gone, she shakily made her way to the bed and sat down, grateful she hadn't simply crumbled to the floor. What kind of a mess had she gotten herself into? Wanting Spencer was like wanting to dance with the devil. She knew that. It wasn't as if she'd misjudged him, or didn't have proof. And yet...

She lay down, pulled the comforter over her clothed body and prayed for sleep.

SPENCER THREW his shirts into his suitcase. He didn't give a damn about the mess he was making, all he wanted to do was get his stuff and get out.

He couldn't believe what he'd done. Of all the damn times to act like a gentleman. He'd had his chance, and he'd blown it, just as he'd blown everything since he'd come back to Maggie.

He should have used the moment. Told Gary that he wasn't going to have Maggie, not tonight, not ever. He should have taken her in his arms and told her all the things that he could do for her now. Forced her to see that he was the man she'd loved once, and still loved, whether she wanted to admit it to herself or not.

Instead, he'd walked away with his tail between his legs like the dog he was. The weak, sniveling fool who'd mastered the art of losing, of throwing away any chance he'd ever had of happiness.

All because he'd been a jerk five years ago. He'd taken a risk that was stupid, for a payoff that was unsure. He'd gambled his last dime because he had nothing to lose. Or so he'd thought. What a joke.

He slammed the closet door and went to the bathroom to get his things in there. Scooping everything up with no mind as to what would break or spill, he filled his kit. He ripped the cord of his electric shaver from the wall, and when it balked, he threw the goddamn thing into the bathtub and listened to the plastic pieces shatter.

Turning away, he caught sight of his reflection. He flicked off the light, not willing to face the man in the mirror. The fool who'd gotten his wish but lost the reason for wishing it in the first place.

All his success meant nothing, worse than nothing. It was his punishment. And he deserved every last dime.

MAGGIE WENT to the guest house at dawn. She hadn't expected him to be there, but when she saw the unmade bed, the open empty drawers, she was disappointed anyway.

She wandered through the rooms until she found the broken shaver in the bathtub. It was the sign she'd been looking for. He'd left in a rage. Just like Gary.

She'd certainly had a busy week.

She wandered back to the living room, and her gaze fell on the vase on the fireplace mantel. It was Baccarat crystal, worth almost a thousand dollars. The flowers in it were real, calla lilies, brought in weekly by the gardeners.

She remembered when she'd gotten the vase. Six months to the day after she'd married Spencer. She'd returned his gift, a clock worth about twenty-two dollars, and bought herself something she wanted more. She remembered the look on his face when she'd told him what she'd done. He'd been so hurt, so crushed.

She'd tried to explain that it didn't matter. She'd loved that he'd thought of her with the clock, but they had so many of them already, and didn't this vase look pretty in their bare apartment? He'd smiled, but not with his eyes. She'd gone on to make dinner, feeling quite pleased that she'd managed the situation so well. He was upset, but only because his feelings were a little hurt that she didn't like his present. It had taken her years to figure out that he'd been ashamed. That he'd gotten her the best thing he could afford. She'd humiliated him, and it hadn't been the first time. It hadn't been the last, either.

Why had she been so slow to grow up? To get wise? Why hadn't she seen back then that the little trinkets she'd wanted so desperately meant absolutely nothing. And that every time she spent her father's money, her husband died a little more inside? She picked up the heavy crystal, feeling the weight of her own humiliation in her hand. She wanted to throw it against the wall, just as he'd smashed his shaver in the tub, but she couldn't even do that. She just put it back, and walked away.

Halfway to the main house, she stopped and stared into the swimming pool. No one would be coming out here, no one was even up. She undid the belt to her robe and let it drop at her feet. Then she slipped out of her nightgown and slippers. Without a second's hesitation, she dived.

It wasn't until she felt the cool grace of the water on her body that she realized she'd been hoping for a baptism, a cleansing of her sins. But nothing was clean, nothing pure. She'd hurt people, and all the swimming in the world wasn't going to fix that. No matter what she did next, she'd hurt someone more. It should have been a happy time, filled with wedding gifts, flower arrangements and honeymoon plans. Instead, she was caught in the middle of a cyclone of her own making.

Of course Spencer shouldn't have come back. It all would have worked out if he'd kept away.

No. She wasn't going to blame him. It was her fault, her mistake that had come back to haunt her.

She dived under the water again, pushing off from the side. Gliding in the silence, she turned off the scolding voice in her head and concentrated on her body. It had been years since she'd gone skinny-dipping. Just another one of her favorite guilty pleasures that she'd ignored in her efforts to become mature and sensible.

What puzzled her now was why she'd ever thought mature and sensible was such a prize? What had it gotten her? Gary. Okay, that was good. Sort of. And then there was her work. Yes. That was worth one hell of a lot.

But who said she couldn't work for the shelters

and skinny-dip? Were they necessarily mutually exclusive? Wasn't the goal to have balance?

She turned onto her back and floated, letting everything in her relax as she closed her eyes.

Balance, that was the key. Work hard, play hard. Laughter and tears. She'd gone from one extreme to the other without missing a beat. Spencer was everything exciting; Gary was everything rational.

Okay, then what was she? What in hell did she want?

She opened her eyes and stared into the blue of the early-morning sky. Somewhere there was an answer. There just had to be.

"WHAT'S THE MATTER, sunshine? You look positively wretched."

Maggie looked up from her lounge chair. Fiona, decked out in a sun hat that could shade the Sudan, a sundress that looked like two scarves stitched together and a see-through pink plastic purse, shook her head in sympathy.

"What are you doing here?" Maggie asked. "I thought you were on your deathbed."

Fiona put down the purse, then climbed gingerly atop the lounge chair next to Maggie's. "It was a miracle. Josh laid his hands on me, and the next thing I knew, I was cured."

"Right," Maggie said, adjusting the suit she'd put on an hour ago, just before she'd called Darlene and told her she couldn't possibly look at flowers today, and that, no, the seating arrangement was not done.

"So tell me everything," Fiona said, adjusting her large round sunglasses. "Leave nothing out."

"I don't want to talk about it."

"Of course you do, sweetie."

Maggie shook her head, determined not to get into the great drama of her life. She closed her eyes behind her sunglasses, took a deep breath. Then she sat bolt upright. "Here's what I'd like to know. I'd like to know why I've ended up being the bad guy. Spencer walks into my life and pulls the rug out from under me, and now Gary is furious with me, and I just want to know how this all happened. Huh?"

"So much for not wanting to talk about it," Fiona said, not even bothering to look surprised at her friend's outburst.

"Will you tell me? What did I do to deserve this? I'm a very nice person, dammit. You know I am. Right?"

"You're a saint, Maggie. Now sit back down so you don't get sun damage." Fiona looked back at the house. "I asked for mimosas. You'd think Cora would realize that mimosas on a weekday constitutes an emergency."

"I don't want to drink," Maggie said, lying back down under the huge white umbrella that covered them both. "I just want to know what to do. Fiona, help me."

"I only wish I could, honey. But I think this is one mess you're going to have to solve on your own."

"That's not helping me."

"You were never happier than when you were with Spencer."

"I was never more miserable, either."

"Gary understands you. He knows the kind of people you come from."

"And he's just as big a snob as I am. How are we supposed to raise decent children when we're both such incredible elitists?"

"Spencer makes you weak in the knees."

"All we have is sex. There's nothing else to build a life on."

"Gary makes you feel safe."

"Safe and dull. Dull as dishwater."

Fiona stripped off her tiny sundress, revealing the smallest bikini in the history of sexy swimwear. She grabbed a giant tube of sunblock and started smearing it on her legs.

"Is that it? You're not going to say any more?"

"Go back to Spencer," Fiona said.

"What? Are you crazy?"

"Get married to Gary," Fiona said with the same inflection.

"You hate me too, don't you?" Maggie threw her hands into the air, but her so-called best friend didn't even have the decency to witness the move. Sighing bitterly, she looked back up at the house. "Didn't you say we had mimosas coming?"

Fiona stopped her ministrations and looked at Maggie. "How long are you going to act like an idiot?"

"Pardon me?"

"You heard me. When are you planning to apologize to Spencer?"

"I—"

"Nothing is going to get cleared up around here until you make amends, darling, and you know it. All this is just a diversionary tactic. You owe it to Spencer, and you owe it to Gary. Dammit, you owe it to yourself. Get your act together, kid, and tell the man you treated him badly because you were afraid."

"I wasn't."

Fiona's mouth went into a thin line.

"All right, so I was afraid."

"And?"

"And I was spoiled."

"And?"

"You know I hate you, right?" Maggie said, wondering how hard it would be to find a new best friend before Friday.

"And?" Fiona said, not letting her off the hook for one second.

"And it was the worst mistake I've ever made."

"Okay," Fiona said, settling back down. "So here's what we do. We apologize to Spencer, we figure out who we really love, and we don't get married until one of our boys is out of our hearts and minds. *Capice?*"

"*Capice.*"

"God, I'm good," Fiona mumbled.

Despite it all, Maggie had to smile. But not for long. Not with what was facing her. Dammit, where were those mimosas?

12

HE'D CANCELED A TRIP to Vegas, a meeting with a new bank, and a dinner with the very attractive hotel general manager. Now Spencer had to decide if he was going to skip the reunion.

He'd purposely checked into the hotel where the party was being held, and now he didn't even know if he wanted to go.

What was he going to do there? Show off? While the idea had appealed a very short time ago, it certainly had lost its charm. He'd discovered something in the past two days: he had been driven all his life by one goal, one lousy goal. Not just the past five years, but his whole life.

He'd striven to acquire enough money to make everyone jealous, to rub their noses in it. Nice. Very nice. It made him proud to be Spencer Daniels.

He got up from his chair and walked over to the phone by the side of the bed. Although the hotel suite was fine, with everything he could want at his fingertips, he'd hated every minute here. Had that inspired him to look for a new house? Or even an apartment? No.

He hadn't done a damn thing since he'd checked in except watch ESPN, order room service and wonder what Maggie was doing. What she was thinking. Whether she was thinking of him.

He'd purposely kept himself out of her way, not even telling Fiona where he'd ended up. Maggie needed time to think, and his presence wasn't going to do anything but mess up the works. The odds were she was going to marry Gary. Spencer gave himself about a five percent chance of coming out ahead. Lousy odds.

But as long as there was any chance at all, he wasn't going to completely disappear. He just needed to regroup, and prepare himself for the inevitable bad news.

Well, there was no time like the present. Tonight, in front of all his ex-classmates, the people who hadn't given him a second thought in high school except to make fun of him, he might as well finish the job.

He sat on the edge of the bed and picked up the phone. But instead of calling Maggie, he dialed Fiona.

It rang for a while, then he heard her breathless, "Hello."

"Hey," he said.

"Where the hell have you been?" Fiona asked.

"Adam's Mark."

"Why haven't you called me?"

"I'm calling you now."

"Do not be a smart-ass," she said, and he could hear the ruffle of material in the background. At least that's what he thought it sounded like. With Fiona, he could never be sure. "I'm having enough trauma tonight without adding you to the list."

"What's wrong?"

"Wrong? Well, let's start with the fact that the dress I was going to wear has some ungodly stain down the right side, and I have no idea where it came from, but I intend to sue the dry cleaners for everything they're worth. You know how I hate to change things at the last minute."

"You're going to look fabulous, Fiona. You always do."

"Thank you," she said, accepting his compliment as her due. "But that's only the beginning."

"What's the rest?"

"Maggie, of course."

"Oh?" he said, trying to keep his voice noncommittal.

"Come on, Spencer. You know you're dying to ask me."

He hesitated, but it was useless. He sighed, fluffed the pillow against the headboard and leaned back. "Give," he said.

"First, she's not going tonight."

"What?"

"At least she's waffling. I told her I'd pick her up at seven, but I'm not sure she's going to go."

"I thought she was going with Gary."

"So did she, until this morning. They've been talking. Long talks. As of last night, the wedding was still on, but the enthusiasm level was less than stellar, if you know what I mean. Then she gets a call this morning. He's going to dinner with a client. He wants her to go with him and skip the reunion. Of course, she says no, that they've been planning this for over a year, but he won't budge. So she tells him no, she's not going to dinner, and he says fine, he's not going to the reunion."

"Fiona?"

"Yes?"

"Don't pick her up."

"I was hoping you were gonna say that."

"Have any pointers for me?"

"Her dress is red, so make sure the flowers go."

"That's not what I meant," he said.

"Oh, that. All I can tell you is that she's been pretty miserable. She doesn't know what to do, Spencer. She's still afraid of you."

"Afraid?"

"Of disappointing you."

"What? She couldn't disappoint me if she tried. She's perfect."

Fiona sighed very dramatically. "Which is exactly the point."

He stared at the phone in his hand, wondering what the hell she was talking about.

"No one is perfect, Spencer," Fiona said. "Not even Maggie. No one can live up to being idolized."

He closed his eyes, the truth and all its repercussions hitting him with one swift blow. "Damn."

"You're welcome. And wear a tux. It's dressy."

"I'll see you tonight," he said, then he hung up the phone. But he didn't get up. He just sat on the bed, listening to the sound of a baseball game coming in a muted whisper from the TV.

FIONA WAS ON TIME, which for Fiona was unheard of. Maggie hadn't even finished putting on her lipstick, or her shoes. She opened the front door, and stopped dead still.

Spencer, in a black tuxedo, holding what looked like several dozen red roses, stood in front of her where Fiona was supposed to be.

He smiled tentatively, and for a moment all she could do was drink in the sight of him, and react. It wasn't an option. She was rooted to the spot, helpless to stop the tightness in her chest, in her stomach and between her legs. She knew she was blushing—she could feel the heat infuse her cheeks, and that wasn't the only place heat pooled. It settled inside her, warming every inch.

"I never got to take you to the prom," Spencer said, his gaze capturing her own. "I'd like to make up for that tonight."

Had he seen what he'd done to her? Could he tell what her body was doing right now—just because it was him?

"I didn't expect you," she said.

"Surprise," he said, looking at her with the same kind of hunger that she knew must be on her own face.

She stepped back. "Come in," she said, although she wasn't sure it was a wise thing to do. She'd guessed she might see him at the reunion, and she'd planned on talking to him in some quiet corner, but his showing up on her doorstep had taken her completely aback.

"I spoke to Fiona," he said. "She told me your date canceled."

Maggie nodded, wondering what else Fiona had told him. Had she mentioned that the plans for the wedding had been put on hold? That she'd asked Gary to wait until she'd figured out what she wanted? Had Fiona repeated the ultimatum that hung over Maggie's head?

"These are for you," Spencer said, holding out the roses.

She took the enormous bouquet from his hand and her fingers brushed his. A shiver raced up her arm, and she realized she'd expected it. It was always that way with Spencer. "They're beautiful," she said.

"Would it be too trite to say they don't hold a candle to you?"

She shook her head. "A compliment like that never gets trite. Let me put them in some water."

He started to follow her to the kitchen, but she stopped him. "Why don't you go get a drink in the library? I'll be ready in a few minutes."

"Of course. Can I fix you something?"

"No, thanks."

He looked at her for a moment more, his gaze moving from her face to her body where it lingered on the curve of her breasts, then back up again. Then he headed for the library, and she returned the favor. She studied him, knocked out with the look of him in the tuxedo. It fit him beautifully, like only an Armani could. He looked like success, and he smelled like confidence, and she could only imagine what the women at the reunion were going to do when they got a load of

him. And how much the other men were going to
hate him.

THE HOTEL BALLROOM was a study in blue and
white, the River Oaks high school colors. Stream-
ers, balloons, floral arrangements, tablecloths, everything matched. Blown-up pictures from the
yearbook dotted the walls, and each round table
had a little plastic tiger mascot bounding out
from the centerpiece.

Maggie followed Spencer to the registration table as she listened to a band work on a very ener-
getic rendition of "Like a Virgin." A lot of people
had arrived before them, perhaps a hundred. The
graduating class had been huge, twice that number. She recognized Penny Kasey sitting behind
the name badges. And there was Kathy Posey
and Don Crane. More and more familiar faces
came into view, although she had to adjust to the
loss of hair, the weight gain, the changes ten years
had brought. The women she'd seen so far all
looked great, better than they had in high school.
The men hadn't fared so well.

"Hey, Maggie," Penny said. "I haven't seen
you in ages. How y'all doing?"

"I'm fine," Maggie said, taking her little name
tag and pasting it on her Valentino gown. "You
look great."

"Thanks," Penny said, but when Maggie
looked up she saw that Penny had more important things to concentrate on than a compliment.

The woman was stricken with Spencer, eating him alive with her gaze.

Maggie saw the other women at the registration table do the same. They were all staring at him as if he were on the dessert menu.

Penny managed to get her hands steady enough to pull out a stick-on name tag. "What's your name, sugar?" she asked, her voice an invitation.

Spencer shook his head. "I'm not a guest. I'm an alumnus."

Penny gave Sandy Weider and Linda Barrett, the other two hungry ladies, a surprised glance. When she faced Spencer again, it was with a dazzling smile. "I can't believe I wouldn't remember you."

"Spencer Daniels," he said.

It took a moment for Penny to remember. But when she did, it was dramatic. Her eyes widened and her mouth popped open into a wide oval. "You're Spencer Daniels? I don't believe it."

"Believe it," Spencer said. Maggie could feel his impatience, and she wanted to tell him to stop and savor the moment. No one had paid attention to Spencer in school, except to call him names or to tease him about his clothes. Now he had the delicious opportunity to rub their collective noses in his success, but all he seemed to want to do was get away from the stares.

He took her arm and led her toward the bar. On the way, he didn't say anything, just walked quickly with his gaze rigidly on his destination. When they finally stopped, he didn't let go of her arm. His fingers dug a little uncomfortably into her, and she touched his shoulder to bring him back to the room.

He looked at her as if he'd only now realized she was by his side. She glanced at his hand, and he let her go quickly. "What can I get you?" he said.

"What was that about?"

"Nothing," he said dismissively. But then he paused. "That's not true. I just realized that I've changed, that's all."

"I think everyone's realized you've changed."

"I'm not talking about that. I mean I used to care about what people like Penny thought. I used to imagine something like this happening. Meeting these people again. What it would feel like when I came back a success."

"How does it feel?"

He shrugged. "Like I spent an awfully long time maneuvering to be king of a castle that was made of air."

She smiled, and took his hand in hers. "Then I'm glad you came."

"Are you?"

She nodded. "Despite everything, yes."

"Ah, but we're talking about the reunion, right? Not about me coming back to you."

Her smile faded as she thought about what she had to tell him. She didn't want to put it off any longer. It was time. Overdue. Glancing around the room, she saw that there was nowhere to talk. The loud music, people milling around in every corner. Suddenly, she didn't want to be here at all. There was only one person she needed to see from her past, and he was standing right next to her.

"How would you feel about leaving for a little while?" she asked.

He grinned. "I'd feel great."

"You don't want a drink first?"

He answered her by taking her hand in his and heading right back to the entrance. The trip wasn't a smooth one, though. Every other step someone said hello to her. She waved back, and tried to be cordial, but Spencer was on a mission. He just kept pulling her through the crowd.

At the door, though, he hesitated. He looked around the room, then at her. "Are you sure? It's your reunion, too. I don't want to spoil it for you."

"We'll come back. I need to meet Fiona here, but we have some time and I have something else to do that's much more important at the moment," she said. "We need someplace quiet and private."

He smiled.

"I DIDN'T KNOW you meant your room, Spencer," Maggie said as he led her inside his suite.

"It's quiet and private. Just what you ordered."

She looked around slowly, but evidently decided that it wasn't such a bad idea after all, because she put her little red purse on the counter and moved directly to the minibar. "I need that drink now," she said. "How about you?"

He nodded. "If you don't see what you like, we'll get it from room service."

She opened the minibar door, studied the array of liquor and beer, then pulled out two small bottles of tequila and a can of orange juice. "Is this okay?"

"Why don't you grab me that Jack Daniel's."

She did, and then she busied herself pouring the drinks into glasses. Finally, she handed him his scotch and took a big sip of tequila. She shivered, then took another.

"Feel better?"

She nodded.

He pointed to the big couch in the living room. "Make yourself comfortable." He decided to do the same, and he took off his jacket and tossed it over the dining-room chair. Next came his tie. After he unbuttoned the top of his shirt, he got his drink and followed her, wondering if this was the beginning of the end, or just the beginning.

He sat down, angling his body so that they were looking at each other. She'd put her drink on the coffee table and was studying her manicure.

"You wanted to talk?" he said.

She nodded, looking up at him. "I wanted to...I should have done this a long time ago."

"Go on," he said softly, encouraging her even though he could see this wasn't easy for her. Frankly, it wasn't easy for him.

She took a deep breath and let it out slowly. She opened her mouth, then closed it again, looked around the room and stood up. "Come with me," she said, taking his hand.

His mood lifted when he saw she was taking him to the bedroom, but when they got to the closet, she stopped and opened the door. It wasn't very roomy. A safe on one side of the floor, in front of that, an ironing board. His clothes were there, too, of course.

Maggie didn't seem to have any qualms about stepping into the small space and pulling him in next to her. Once they were situated, and after he'd pushed two of his suits to the side, she closed the door, leaving them in the dark.

He touched her face, but she guided his hand down to his side. "This isn't what you think," she whispered, as if they were hiding. "I just have to say some things and it's easier in here where I don't have to see you."

His stomach tightened again. He felt as if he'd been in the front car of a roller coaster all evening, and if his luck was any indicator, this is where he was going down. Only this coaster had no brakes.

Maggie cleared her throat. "I was wrong about that résumé," she said, her words coming out in a rush. "I thought at the time I was trying to help you, but I think that was an excuse. Only I wasn't clear until now what I really intended when I made up all those lies about you."

Spencer hadn't expected this. He'd been certain she'd wanted to tell him that she'd made up her mind to marry Gary, and that she didn't want to see him again. He never imagined they were going to revisit one of the most painful experiences of his life. One where he had more to be ashamed of than her.

"For a long time, I thought I was just naive," she hurried on, "that I'd acted impulsively, but that if you hadn't come home so early that night, I'd have torn up the résumé myself."

"And you don't think so anymore?"

"No. Now I think I would have left it on the table so you would have had to find it."

"I see."

"No, Spencer, I don't think you do. It wasn't malicious. At least I didn't intend it to be. I think I knew, before I typed the first word, how you would react. I knew that it would be the final straw. That you would leave me if you read it."

"I knew you wanted me to leave," he said, not telling her that the pain of that knowledge still haunted him.

"Not consciously," she said. "But yes, I did. I wasn't ready for you, Spencer. I was too young, and I was too insecure. I couldn't live up to what you thought of me. And before it all went to hell, I needed you to go. I just didn't know how to do it right. Spencer, it was all my fault. I tried to be the person you wanted me to be and when I failed, I made you feel horrible enough to leave."

Of all the things she could have said... She'd caught him completely off guard—all his defenses, all the words he'd prepared over and over again, were useless. How was it possible that she'd made him feel worse?

"I'm sorry," she said. "I know I hit you below the belt. That I took away your pride. I was cruel and I was spoiled. You didn't deserve any of it."

"Oh, Christ, Maggie. It wasn't you. Don't you

know that? It was me. I should have been the man you created on that résumé. I should have done all those things."

He felt her hands on his face, her fingers finding his lips and covering them gently. "No, that's not true. You were always good enough. I didn't want you to be anything different. I wanted to be worthy of your love."

He heard her sigh as if she'd been holding her breath for a long time.

"It's such a relief to tell you this. I've held it in for so long. But now that I can finally see it, really see it, I know that I'm not such a horrible person. I was wrong, but it wasn't because I was bad, so much as foolish. I let everything get all tangled up because I was young, too young."

He moved her fingers away, although she didn't let his face go. "Maggie—"

His words were cut off by her lips on his. He felt the tears on her cheeks and her relief in the way her hands moved to his back and held him so tight.

He tried to stop her, to tell her, but he couldn't. He couldn't stop kissing her, tasting her, and he knew that no kiss would be enough. That he had to have her in his arms again, in his bed. He had to be inside this woman one more time.

One last time.

He knew it would be the last. Because he had to tell her his own truth. Especially now, when she'd been so honest with him. When it had hurt her so much to say it all.

She'd hate him after he told her. He hated himself for knowing that he didn't care. He threw
open the closet door, lifted her in his arms and
carried her to his bed.

13

MAGGIE STARED UP at Spencer as he lay her down on the clean blue bedspread. Her breath came in great gasps, as if she had just run a great distance, which she supposed she had.

His face, so strong and so beautiful, only inches away, was a study in conflict. The lust there matched her own, but she saw doubt, hesitation.

Then she noticed a small scar, right by his temple, one she'd studied with great attention years before and remembered now as a marker of their past. She knew the story of that scar, and the stories of all the scars that didn't show. Despite all the hurt, despite knowing his scars, she loved him. And seeing the way he looked at her now, with the passion and concern and the blatant *need*, she knew he loved her. Despite her scars. Or maybe because of them.

She lifted her hand to the back of his head, luxuriating in the familiar feel of his thick, dark hair. "Kiss me," she whispered.

"Are you sure?" he asked, his voice a low growl of need.

"I'm sure," she said, moving her free hand to his chest. "I'm quite sure."

"What about…?"

She closed her eyes for a moment, but she didn't need to think about it any further. She knew her answer—at least, part of it. "I'm not going to marry Gary," she said. "As for the rest of it, we'll have to see."

"Oh, Maggie." He leaned down, kissing her with the intensity that had always existed between them. From the first—through all the trouble, and now through the healing—the heat, the craving, had been the constant. She let herself go, trusting her body, trusting her decision for the first time in years.

His tongue slipped between her teeth, teasing her, tasting her, and she tasted him back, a rush of pleasure coursing through her, settling in the heat between her legs.

He must have felt the same powerful urge, because he broke the kiss to sit up, to unbutton his shirt with frantic fingers. She reached down for the bottom of her gown and started lifting it, but he put his hands on hers. "Wait," he said. Although it was terribly difficult not to do something, she obeyed, concentrating on watching him undress.

He slipped off the bed, his gaze never leaving hers as he took off his shirt, revealing the most perfect chest in the world. Well-muscled, sculpted by a master, with a light feathering of dark hair. Her fingers itched to touch him, her mouth yearned to tease his nipples until they were hard little buds in her mouth.

The sound of his zipper brought her gaze down, and she watched him step out of his pants and underwear. His readiness was very apparent. She remembered that, too—the feel of silk over stone. The hot thickness. The taste and scent that marked him as pure male.

Her own readiness was just as apparent and she shifted, squeezing her legs together to ease the pressure. But there was only one thing that would cure her.

Spencer reached over, slipped one hand behind her neck and the other behind her knees. He lifted her for a second, repositioning her on the big bed so that she was right in the middle, with her head on the pillow. Then he climbed up beside her. She thought he was going to kiss her, but he didn't. Instead, he moved down to the bottom of the bed, took the hem of her red gown and inched it up her legs. Slowly, he raised the material, revealing her legs, her knees, her thighs. She heard him gasp as he realized she hadn't worn panty hose, but a garter belt and stockings.

"Oh, Maggie," he whispered, leaving the hem of her dress just at the juncture of her thighs. He leaned down and kissed the exposed flesh above her stocking tops, first on her right leg, then her left.

He used his tongue to explore the small strip of skin, teasing her as he dipped down to the warmth just below her red panties.

She moaned and reached for his head, but he captured her hands and put them back down beside her, letting her know unequivocally that this was his show. He kissed the curve of her thigh once more, then took the hem of her dress.

He raised it slowly, reverently. She watched his eyes as he looked at her, and she saw her own beauty reflected in his gaze.

How could she feel anything less than beautiful when he wanted her so much?

She felt the cool air caress her tummy, and then the shiver of his fingers as they traced the edge of the material from her belly button to the slim bands that held the panties on her hips.

As his thumbs went beneath the cloth, his gaze captured hers. His lips narrowed and his nostrils flared, and at that second he ripped the material, tearing the garment from her body in one powerful move, raising her hips, baring her flesh.

Yet it wasn't enough for him. He lowered his hands to her knees once more and spread her legs. He still hadn't looked down. He hadn't let her look away. The tie between them was as strong as steel, and he held the leash. Moving up so his legs curled under him, rested perfectly between her wide-spread thighs, he let her go. His gaze moved down her body slowly and she felt his anticipation as he finally saw what he'd laid bare.

His soft words were only a murmur, indistinct but so clear in their meaning she felt herself tremble at her power over him. With the dress bunched at her waist, her black high heels still on her feet, her stockings still attached to the garter belt, Maggie had never felt so naked. So deliciously wanton.

She squeezed back a trickle of her own moisture as Spencer bent down, as if he were in prayer. His breath warmed the small V of her hair, and then it was his lips there, making her moan and tense and ache so that everything in the world disappeared but her body, his body, their need.

He took his time, making her squirm beneath his ministrations, making her beg and weep as he explored her very core with his tongue and his fingers. Bringing her to the very brink, but not letting her go over the edge.

How had she lived without this? How had she denied this part of her when it was so strong it threatened to drive her mad? No longer able to keep her hands at her sides, she touched his head, but it was the wrong thing to do, because he stopped.

He sat up, his eyes dark with desire. He took her hands in his and pulled her up so she was sitting, then before she could even react, he reached down, gathered her dress in his hands and pulled it over her head. He smiled as he saw the red bra, lacy and delicate, that matched the garter belt. She arched her back, wanting him to take it off her. His hands went to her breasts and he cupped them for a moment. But only a moment. The next instant, he found the clasp, opened it and peeled the material away as if opening a present.

He cupped her again, squeezing her flesh gently, then he bent down so he could swirl his tongue around her nipple. She felt the pressure, the ache of constriction as he captured the bud between his teeth and suckled.

Her hands went down his back, running over

his smooth hard flesh. "Please, Spencer," she begged. "Let me taste you."

He lifted his head and kissed her on the mouth, ignoring her plea. Finally, he broke the kiss, stared at her for a moment, then took her hand and guided it down his stomach, through the wiry hair, all the way until she grasped his flesh in her hand. Hard, hot, pulsing with the rhythm of his heart, she let her hand explore, remembering the feel of every inch.

His moan came from deep inside. "I need you," he whispered. "Now."

"But…"

"No. We can do that later. I can't stand it. I have to be inside you."

She released him and she lowered her head back down to the pillow.

He stayed on his knees, looking at her body once more, then his hands went beneath her knees and he lifted her legs up and back. Moving as slowly and powerfully as a jungle cat, he aligned his body with hers, teasing her with the feel of the tip of him at her entrance.

"Maggie," he whispered as he thrust into her.

She gasped, cried out as he filled her completely. As he made her complete.

Guiding her legs around him, she gripped him tightly. He moved his hands up, balancing on his elbows, bringing her the lips she needed, the kisses that swallowed her moans.

He thrust into her over and over, deeper and deeper, and she ran her hands over him, touching everything she could, wanting him closer still. He kissed her neck, gently bit the lobe of her ear. Then she heard his whisper. "Maggie," he murmured, so close that his breath made her shiver. "I love you so much. I've never stopped loving you. What did I do, letting you go?"

She reached up and took his head in her hands, moving his mouth to hers. She kissed him deeply, then found his gaze. "You're the only man I've ever loved," she said. "The only man I've been with. Or wanted to be with."

He groaned, his eyes closing and his thrusts growing more urgent. She watched his face contort into the mask of pleasure that looked so much like pain. She felt her insides clench tighter as the friction built and built, and then she climaxed in a burst of trembling ecstasy. As she cried out, she heard his voice, felt him embed himself inside her again, and she held him as he rode to his release.

For a long moment, he just stayed still. She continued to quiver as wave after wave of satisfaction surged through her body, her contractions around him eliciting soft groans.

Finally, he looked at her once more, and he smiled. His pleasure and hers a shared triumph, a secret between them.

"I don't ever want to move," he said. "I want to stay right here for the rest of my life."

"I agree," she said. "Although it could become a little tricky in a week or two."

He sighed, letting his head drop to her shoulder. "We'll work it out. Trust me."

Her hands traversed his back, and although she hated to admit defeat, she had to lower her legs.

But he didn't pull away. He just shifted a tiny bit, enough for her to tug him back in with her muscles.

"Tell me something," he said, his mouth very close to her ear so all he had to do was whisper. "Was it always like this? I remember it being great, but not this great."

She grinned. "I think you're right. And my memory is pretty good."

"Oh God," he groaned. "I have to move. I don't want to move, but I have to move."

"If you must," she said, squeezing him a last time.

He eased out of her with a soft hiss of pleasure, then turned so he lay next to her on the bed. "You think room service would mind if I asked them to bring us each a glass of water?"

"We'd have to make sure the waiter was blindfolded, but I think the idea has merit."

He laughed, a warm, intimate sound that choked her up for a second. Then he got up and walked out of the bedroom. She watched him the whole way, loving the sight of his naked back, especially the lower quadrant.

She hugged herself, then kicked her shoes off so they went flying across the room. All her dilemmas were gone. Not her problems, but her questions. Her uncertainty. She was exactly where she belonged. Back with the only man she'd ever really loved.

Of course, she had to speak to Gary. That wouldn't be very pleasant. Through it all, she'd never stopped liking him, but tonight she'd seen so clearly that it had always been *liked* with Gary. Not loved. She'd gone to him because he was safe, and she hadn't felt very brave.

But she felt brave now. She was able to look at her accomplishments and be proud of them. She knew her shortcomings, too, but they weren't overwhelming anymore. She wasn't perfect, but she was damn good.

Confessing to Spencer had been a cleansing. A rebirth. She'd had no idea how much of her self-worth had been tied up in that one moment. How many doubts had been born all those years ago, and how she'd nurtured those doubts until she'd lost all perspective.

Now she wanted to move forward. She wanted to be with Spencer, love him, grow with him. And she wanted it all right now.

He walked back into the room holding two glasses of water. His smile warmed her like no blanket could. She took her glass and drank greedily. When she looked at Spencer, he was grinning at her again.

"What?"

"You know, as far as reunions go, I think this just might be the best that ever was."

Maggie sat up so quickly she spilled the little bit of water left in the glass all over the bed. "Oh, God. Fiona!"

"Pardon?"

"What time is it?" Maggie scooted to the side of the bed. She found her dress, and one of her shoes.

"It's just past ten."

"Thank God. Fiona's downstairs. She's waiting for us."

"She can wait."

"No, it's important," she said, grabbing his hand. "Come on, let's get in the shower. We have to get down there."

MAGGIE WAS SURE Fiona was going to kill her for being so late. But once she understood...

The party was in full swing when they reentered the ballroom. The band played "Holiday," and Maggie wondered if they knew anything except Madonna tunes.

"Do you see her?" Spencer asked, leaning close and speaking loudly to be heard over the noise.

Maggie shook her head. "If I know Fiona, she's probably by the bar."

"There are three stations," he said. "You want to go clockwise, or straight down the middle?"

She took his hand and led him to the left. All along the perimeter of the dance floor were the buffet tables, with a narrow aisle banked on the other side by small round tables. She really hadn't expected this big a turnout. Everywhere she looked there was someone else she hadn't seen in ages, and she decided that once she found Fiona, she'd spend some time mingling. Not too long, though, as she had a new hobby.

Smiling as she remembered the effort and willpower it had taken them both to shower and not play, she let her gaze wander over the crowd, searching for the unmistakable silhouette of

Fiona Drake, who was certain to be in the thick of things.

She'd been a wild girl in high school, and had made just as many enemies as friends. Maggie could well imagine that not too many of the girls, at least the girls she'd hung out with, would be happy to see how beautiful Fiona still was. And that she still attracted men like metal to a magnet.

Spencer pulled on her arm and she stopped, following his gaze to a young woman she didn't recognize. Rather plain and plump, the blond woman stared at Spencer with a shy smile.

"Who's that?" Maggie asked.

"It's Laura Abrams," Spencer said. "She was a good friend once. One of the few. We used to spend a lot of time together."

Maggie let go of his hand. "Go on," she said. "I'll find Fiona."

Spencer leaned down and kissed her on the cheek. "I won't be long, but I do want to talk to her."

"It's fine. I'll find you."

He smiled, kissed her once more, then headed for his friend. Maggie's eyes were drawn to the circle of women standing to the right of Laura Abrams. Penny was there, as well as a number of the other popular girls. Ex-cheerleaders, a home-coming queen, a class vice president. They'd been *the* group—the girls who'd set the tone, and made the rules. Maggie had been on the periphery of that action, and it was only Fiona who had kept her out of the very worst of the socializing. But now, none of the women had noticed her at all.

Their focus was entirely on Spencer. She could understand it. Without prejudice she could say that he was the best-looking man in the room. He'd always had charisma, and now that he'd grown into the full bloom of powerful manhood, no one could let him pass without notice.

Even the guys had their eyes on him. Jimmy Fallon, Penny's one-time boyfriend, studied Spencer as if he were the enemy. No one had liked Spencer in high school, and it must be quite a blow to the egos of all the ex-jocks to see him waltz in like a king. Jimmy leaned over to Carl somebody, and they whispered for a moment, then laughed. From the look on their faces, the joke had been particularly cruel.

She found Spencer again. He had moved with Laura to the edge of the dance floor. The two of them were doing a slow dance. Spencer smiled at her, but Laura kept her head down. They weren't terribly close to each other, and they weren't very elegant, but Maggie could feel the tenderness of the moment from across the room.

Almost as a reflex, she checked back on Penny and the girls. They clearly couldn't feel anything but jealousy. Penny whispered something to Robin Popp, the ex–homecoming queen, then the two of them started toward Spencer and Laura. As soon as they started walking, Maggie did, too.

She'd almost caught up to them when she heard her name called. Turning around, she saw Fiona waving frantically. Maggie waved back, signaling Fiona to join her, then she turned back.

Penny and her gang were on one side of Spencer and Laura, Jimmy and Carl on the other. Maggie could see Spencer look for a way to get Laura out of there, but they were trapped.

"You look great, Laura," Penny said, smiling broadly, dripping insincerity. "Can you believe that this is Spencer? We were all just saying that he's a shoo-in for most successful, weren't we?"

The girls behind her nodded, and Laura's face turned pink. She stopped dancing and tried to get away, but Spencer held on to her hand. He looked down at her, ignoring the crowd around him. "Would you like a drink?"

Maggie turned toward them, meaning to guard Laura's other side as they got out of there, but someone grabbed her arm, stopping her short. She turned. "Let me go, Fiona."

"Maggie," she said, her smile broad, but her eyes filled with urgency. "Look who I brought. Isn't it a nice surprise?"

"In a minute, Fiona," she said, trying to shake her off.

"It's Gary," Fiona said, and Maggie stopped. There, right behind Fiona, Gary stood with his arms crossed, his gaze moving from Maggie to Spencer and back again. He looked cool and elegant in his tuxedo, his Rolex reflecting the light from the mirrored ball on the ceiling.

Behind her, she heard Jimmy, his voice loud and slurred. "Hey, look," he said. "Daniels finally got himself a pair of new shoes. Whaddaya know."

"Stop it, Jimmy," Penny said. "I've read all

about him. He's very successful now. He was in *Forbes,* for your information."

"*Forbes,* huh? What did you do, marry some rich broad?"

Maggie turned away from Gary. She had to stop this. It was all the things she'd hated about high school, all the things that she knew had been part of herself for so long. The rigid class prejudice, the way she'd felt so damn superior to anyone who had less.

"Excuse me," Spencer said, pushing his way past Jimmy, holding on to Laura's shoulder.

"Hey," Jimmy said. "You might be Mr. Forbes now, but you can't hide what you were. Everyone knew that your father was a drunk. That you didn't have a pot to piss in. How they let you in our school is beyond me."

"Stop it," Maggie said. "Spencer, let's go."

"That's right," Jimmy said. "I remember now. You two were married, weren't you?" He looked at Spencer again, his disgust evident on his reddened face. "So that's how you did it, right? Alimony?"

"No, that's not how he did it."

Maggie turned at the sound of Gary's voice. He'd joined them, although he knew only two of the players. Fiona was right behind him, pulling him back, but he didn't budge.

"But I know how he did," Gary continued. "Why don't you tell them, Spencer? Why don't you tell us all how you got that job at Merrill Smith?"

Maggie didn't understand. She looked from

Gary to Spencer, and then froze. Spencer's face had changed. He wasn't paying attention to anyone but her now. He'd even let go of Laura's hand. It was his eyes that made her stomach clench. A look of remorse so great that it made her go cold all over.

"Maggie," he said.

"Go on, Spencer," Gary said. "Tell her."

"No," Fiona said, stepping between Gary and Maggie. "Let's all just leave now, okay?"

"I want to hear this," Jimmy said, but Maggie dismissed him. What she couldn't dismiss was Spencer's hesitation. The guilt she saw on his face.

"What is it?" she whispered, afraid to know.

He came over to her and took her hands in his. "I didn't want you to hear it like this. I wanted to wait until tonight. Until we were alone."

"What, for God's sake?"

He dropped her hands. "I didn't tear up that phony résumé you wrote. I took it. I used it. It's how I got my first job."

14

MAGGIE HEARD JIMMY say something about how people never change, and then laughter. The band started playing "Celebrate," and someone took flash pictures across the room. But that was outside. Inside, only one thing happened. The last five years of her life came up and slapped her in the face.

"Let's go," Spencer said. "I'd like to explain."

"Explain what?" she said, digging deep to find the charming Southern smile that had been drilled into her psyche since birth.

"Please, Maggie, this is no place—"

"This is the perfect place for the truth to come out. It's a reunion, isn't it? The time for revisiting the past? For looking back at the decisions we made, and gauging their effectiveness?"

She knew his hand was on her arm, but it felt strangely disconnected. Then Gary moved right next to them, taking her other arm.

"She's coming with me," he said. "I think you've done enough for one night."

Maggie wanted to jerk her arms free, but once more, her training came into play. Still smiling, she gently turned toward the exit. Spencer let go. Gary didn't. She looked down at where he held her for a long pregnant moment. Then he, too, let her go.

Fiona stood in front of her, concern marring her perfect features. "Come on, Maggie."

"Where?"

"Out," Fiona said as she maneuvered herself behind her and started shepherding her toward the door.

Maggie didn't argue. She was too busy thinking about what she'd just heard, remembering the afternoon that Spencer had found the phony résumé. None of the lies had been blatant. He'd gone to the University of Texas, instead of Wharton, and he hadn't earned his master's. He had worked at her father's bank, but as a clerk, not a loan executive. He'd never belonged to the political or social organizations she'd given him credit for, or belonged to the fraternity that marked him as a wealthy young man from a good background. They were the kinds of lies that would be cause for instant dismissal if discovered.

Spencer had been livid. He'd told her that he'd always known she didn't think he was good enough for her, that he didn't need her duplicity to get a job. Even if she didn't believe in him, he would still make it. Make it on his brains and his talent. That he'd had nothing his whole damn life, that he'd had to fight for anything decent. Mostly, she remembered how he'd told her he was leaving. That he'd divorce her so she could find someone with blue enough blood, with a big enough bank account. But that one day he'd be back, and he'd show her.

Well, that part had come true. He'd come back. And he'd shown her.

A man carrying several drinks bumped into her shoulder, knocking her back to the present. They were almost at the door, and she had to fight the urge to run.

Finally, they cleared the last hurdle, and she stood with Fiona in the hotel lobby. When she turned, she saw that Gary and Spencer had followed. Both men looked at her, one in triumph, one in disgrace.

She wasn't going to put it off. Not this. Not tonight.

She looked at Fiona and Spencer. "Would you two excuse us for a moment?"

She took Gary's hand and led him to an empty corner couch. They sat, his knees touching hers. She focused on his face, really seeing him. The man she'd run to for safety, whom she'd hidden behind so that she wouldn't risk her heart.

"Maggie—"

She held up her hand. "Please, don't. I want to get this out right. I don't think it would be a very good idea for us to get married. Not because of what just happened, and not because of anything you've done. It's just not there between us. It never has been."

He started to protest, but she quieted him with a kiss on the cheek. "You know it's the truth. There's never been more than a kinship, a friendship that I've treasured. But it was never love. Never the kind of love that would have satisfied either of us."

She thought he was going to argue, but he didn't. Actually, he looked a little relieved. His gaze went back to Spencer, then Fiona. He looked at her for a long time. Then he came back to her. "I'm sorry," he said.

"For what? You didn't do anything wrong. You've been a perfect gentleman."

He laughed. "So that's what I did wrong, huh?"

She smiled, touched his cheek. "No, you did that right. And you deserve to have someone who appreciates all the things you are, and loves you with all the passion in the world."

"We both deserve that," he said.

She nodded. "Yes, we do."

He looked back at Spencer again. "Is it him?"

"It was," she confessed. "But now, I don't know."

"You needed to know the truth," he said. "I'm sorry it hurt you, but…"

"I did need to know, although, frankly, I would have preferred hearing it another way."

He looked down, frowning. "I had to try. I do care about you."

"Yes," she said. "I know."

"So what are you going to do?"

"Go home. Get some sleep. Tomorrow is going to be pretty busy. There'll be my mother's stroke, and Darlene's heart attack," she said, only exaggerating a little.

"Is there anything I can do?"

She shook her head. "Just let your family know. I'll do the rest. But now I need to talk to Spencer."

"I'll wait. Take you home."

"No, don't. Thanks, but don't. Did you bring Fiona?"

He nodded.

"Take her home. And let her be your friend. She'll be there for you if you let her."

He smiled, an unexpected smile. One Maggie wasn't sure she understood. "I've found that out," he said. "We've been on the phone a lot lately."

"I'm glad," Maggie said.

Gary found her hand and squeezed it, then he leaned over and kissed her very sweetly on the lips. A tender goodbye. She watched him stand, walk over to Fiona and Spencer. They spoke for a moment, then Gary took Fiona's arm and they headed for the exit.

Spencer headed for her.

Gary didn't even look at him when he walked past. But that wasn't what concerned Spencer now. What did was that Maggie had gotten up and was heading toward the lobby.

He hurried, but she was moving as fast as she could in those high heels of hers. When he finally caught up to her, she was inches from the door. He touched her arm, and she flinched, but at least she stopped.

"Spencer, I can't talk to you right now, okay? Maybe tomorrow, but not tonight."

"I understand," he said. "I just…I'm so sorry."

She didn't move. She didn't even look at him. "Would you have told me?" she asked quietly.

"Yes," he said. "I was going to tell you tomorrow."

"Why tomorrow?"

"Because I'm selfish. I wanted you to love me for one whole night."

She finally looked up, and he almost wished she hadn't. His betrayal was like a wound that had gone beneath her skin. That had damaged her forever.

"I won't deny it was a lousy thing that I did," he said. "And I'll also admit that, until a few days ago, I had no intention of telling you. But that changed. Being with you changed me."

He stepped closer to her, but he still didn't touch her. He wouldn't, until she gave him her consent. But it killed him not to. "I came back to Houston with only one thing in mind. To make you sorry you ever let me go. To make you pay."

"Congratulations," she said. "Mission accomplished."

He shook his head. "I'm trying to tell you. It changed. It changed so quickly I didn't know what to do with myself. I touched you, and I knew I couldn't hurt you any more than I already had. I kissed you, and I knew that I'd never stopped loving you, not even for a day. Maggie, I want you back. I want to marry you."

She stepped away as if he'd slapped her. "You want to marry me? You put me through hell. Five long years of guilt and remorse, and blaming myself for being a horrible wife, and a lousy snob. And all that time, you... I can't talk about this tonight. If you care anything about me, you'll let me go."

There was nothing left for him to do. He just nodded his defeat, and watched her walk out of the hotel. Out of his life.

He'd come for revenge, but all he'd gotten was bitter disappointment, and the terrible knowledge that it was completely his fault. He'd just lied to Maggie—he hadn't changed at all. He was still a mongrel, still a fraud, and now more than ever, he knew he didn't deserve her. He never had.

"DADDY? Do you have a minute?"

Maggie's father looked up from the book he was reading, placing a finger on the spot where he'd left off. She'd seen the library light on when she'd walked in, had debated going right to bed, but she knew she wouldn't sleep. And she knew she needed advice.

"How was your party?" he said, smiling his welcome.

She entered the library, closing the door behind her, pausing beside the closet where… "It was interesting."

"Oh?" he said, closing the book. "Tell me about it."

She went over to the couch, slipped off her heels and curled herself into the corner. She'd always liked talking to her father when he was in here. She'd even bought him a smoking jacket once, but he only wore it a few times, preferring the comfortable robe he had on now.

"I called off the wedding," she said, deciding that it was too late for equivocation.

"That is interesting."

"And Spencer asked me to marry him again."

"This was some reunion."

She smiled, but it didn't last. Her chin trembled, and she blinked back tears. When her father handed her the box of tissues, she didn't blink quite so hard.

"What did you tell Spencer?" he asked.

"I told him I didn't want to talk about it." She wiped under her eyes and sniffed. "Daddy, he took the résumé. He used it. That's how he got his job, by using the lies that I told, that he left me for."

"I see," he said calmly.

"You don't seem very surprised."

"I'm not. I've known about that for a long time."

He couldn't have said anything that would have surprised her more. Oh, maybe that he'd suggested that Spencer use the phony document, but she knew her father too well for that. He was the most ethical man she'd ever met. "How? Why didn't you tell me?"

"First," he said, "it was told to me in confidence. Now that you know, I don't see the harm in admitting it, but I couldn't before. I wouldn't have, even if he hadn't asked me to keep it quiet."

"Why?"

"Because this was something you two needed to work out. He needed to tell you, but before that, you needed to apologize to him. Mistakes were made. My interference wouldn't have corrected any of them."

"But I'm your daughter!"

"Precisely why it was so important for me to keep quiet. I couldn't fix this one for you, sweetheart. You had to see for yourself, make your own choices."

"But how did you find out?"

Frank hesitated, and she knew he was deciding whether to tell her the truth or not. He wouldn't lie, but he might decide that it was something else she needed to find out on her own. "Spencer called me about three and a half years ago. He asked me if I'd read a letter he'd written, and give him any suggestions on how he could make it better."

Maggie sniffed again, but her tears had stopped completely. "Did Mother know?"

He chuckled. "No. It was just between Spencer and myself."

"Go on," she said. "What was in the letter?"

"It was his resignation from Merrill Smith. It was his confession and apology."

"What?" She sat back, completely taken by surprise.

"He hadn't been able to live with it, even though his performance was outstanding. He couldn't go on with the lie. He told them, and he left, and at that time I don't believe he had any idea that he would be able to make a living. Strong stuff for a man who grew up with nothing."

"But why did he use the résumé in the first place?"

"Why did you write it?"

"Because I was young and scared and foolish."

Frank nodded.

She sat for a moment, tearing her tissue into tiny little pieces. "That still doesn't excuse it. And it doesn't excuse his not telling me."

"He did. Probably a little later than he should have, but I knew when he walked through our front door that he was going to tell you. I could only hope that he'd wait long enough for you to take care of your end of this business."

"This is so Machiavellian. I can't believe you knew all this and you didn't say anything."

"My daughter's happiness was at stake. I had to move carefully."

"So why are you telling me this now?"

"Because, unless I'm very much mistaken, I think you're in love with Spencer."

She sighed. "God, you should get your own extension at the Psychic Friends Network."

He laughed. "It wasn't that hard to figure out, Maggie. He walked in, and you became someone else. No, I said that wrong. You became Maggie again."

"Poor Gary," she said.

"He'll land on his feet, don't you worry about him."

"I'm still scared, Daddy. I don't know what to do."

"I'm not telling you to marry Spencer. You have to make up your own mind about that.

Whatever you decide, your mother and I will support you completely."

Maggie's eyes widened. "Mother will support me if I go back to Spencer?"

"She will. Eventually. But that's not what's important. You're the one who has to live your life. You have to choose the direction."

"I hate choosing."

He gave her a smile, and it was so filled with love and affection that she teared up all over again. "For what it's worth, I think what Spencer did took an extraordinary amount of courage. He made a mistake. We all do that. But very few of us admit it and make it right. Whatever success he has today he made completely on his own merit."

"We spent some time together tonight," she said, taking another tissue. "Alone. It was wonderful, but you know, I still think he puts me on that pedestal."

"He knows you're human, sweetheart, but I don't think he'll ever take you down from that perch. I'd think less of him if he did."

"Can I live up to it?"

"I think it would make a very worthy goal."

She stood up and went to her father's chair. Leaning over, she kissed him on the cheek, then kissed him again for good measure. "Thanks, Dad. I appreciate...everything."

"I'm glad I could help," he said. "It's late. It's time we both went to bed."

"I'll go up in a bit," she said.

He rose and walked her to the door. "Follow

your instincts, Maggie," he said. "They're de-
pendable."

She watched him for a while, and once he was
gone, she thought about going to the kitchen or
going to bed. Neither felt right. Instead, she went
to the back door and headed to the pool.

The balmy air helped immediately. It calmed
her nerves and settled her thoughts. As she
walked to the pool, things clicked into place, and
by the time she reached the edge she'd made her
decision.

She would marry Spencer.

She would live with him again, only this time,
on equal footing. With all this experience behind
them, knowing how fragile the relationship was,
and tending to it carefully.

She'd be there for his successes and his failures.
Know his support would always be right there for
her.

They'd have babies who would have his eyes.
His humor. His strength.

She stared at the water, rippling ever so gently,
the lights wavering ethereally on the bottom. A
shadow appeared on the water right next to her
own. A strong, beautiful shadow. A man standing so tall.

"I couldn't go," Spencer said. "I couldn't walk
away this time. Maggie, what I did was wrong. I
made a terrible mistake."

She turned and looked up into his dark blue
eyes. This was the man she would grow old with.
Who she'd care for and laugh with. Make love
with.

"Why are you smiling?" he asked, his confusion making him all the more appealing.

"Because I know something you don't."

"What's that?"

"I know that you and I are going to be incredibly happy."

"We are?"

She nodded. "We're going to have three or four kids. A dog and a cat. We're going to buy a house together. Go on vacations and to baseball games. And we're going to spend an awful lot of time in the bedroom."

"It sounds perfect," he said, taking her hands in his. "But what about…"

"Here's the thing that I learned, Spencer. It takes a long time to grow up. Maybe all our lives. But I'd like to grow up with you at my side. What do you think?"

"I think you're the most incredible woman in the entire world," he said. "Almost a goddess."

She put her hands on her hips. "I thought we'd been over that."

"I said *almost*. I had to take points off for snoring."

"I don't snore!"

"Ahh, Maggie," he said, his voice tender and sweet and filled with humor. "It's very, very cute snoring."

She sighed. "I think you'd better kiss me."

And he did.

_____ Epilogue _____

Nine months later

MAGGIE SHIFTED, trying to get more comfortable as she listened to the preacher. It was important to pay attention as he said the vows, but the pain in her back was getting worse. She glanced at Spencer, sitting in the second row. His gaze was on hers, concern marring his features. She smiled at him, hoping to ease his worry, but it didn't work.

She turned her attention back to the altar. Fiona looked so beautiful in her Vera Wang wedding dress. And Gary seemed happier than she'd ever known him.

It was almost over. Gary slipped the ring on Fiona's finger, and they said the words that made them husband and wife. None too soon, either. Because the next pain Maggie felt was unmistakable.

Not wanting to distract from her best friend's moment, she plastered a smile on her face and waited until it was her cue to give Fiona her bouquet. After a very long kiss between the bride and groom, she finished her duties as matron of honor and watched the two of them walk down the aisle.

Before they'd gone halfway, Spencer was at her side. "Are you okay?"

"I think we're going to miss the reception," she said.

"Are you kidding?"

She shook her head.

"Oh, damn. Okay. I'll go get the car. You stay here."

"I think I'd better sit down."

He walked her toward the pews, and then her parents and Caroline gathered around her. "It's time," Spencer said.

"Oh, heavens," Betty said, sitting down next to her. "Someone get the car."

Caroline sat on her other side looking worried and excited. Her father just looked worried.

"Watch her," Spencer said, then he darted down the aisle, making his way through the crowd.

"I don't want to ruin Fiona's wedding," Maggie said.

"Nothing's going to be ruined," her mother said. "You just relax."

"But you all need to be at the reception."

"The reception can wait," a female voice called out.

Maggie looked behind her to see Fiona approaching. "What are you doing here?" she asked. "Go get pelted with rice."

"That can wait, too," Betty said.

"Are you joking?" Fiona said. "Is it…?"

"Yes!" Maggie said, her voice rising unnaturally as another contraction hit. When it passed, she shook her head. "I'm fine. Go have a party."

"We'll have the party later. Now we have to get you to the hospital."

"Please, Fiona. I love you, and I don't want you to take this the wrong way, but get the hell out of here."

"If I didn't know Spencer was going to take such good care of you…"

"Yeah, yeah. Go on. Save me some cake."

Fiona leaned down, pushed her veil out of the way and kissed her on the cheek. "Be safe," she said. "We'll come to the hospital as soon as we can get away."

"Go on your honeymoon."

"And miss the birth of my godchild? Not likely."

"There they are," Caroline said.

Maggie turned to see Spencer and Gary hurrying toward her. Despite the aching and the nervous excitement, she felt an indescribable calm settle over her. It was all perfect. Fiona and Gary, so much in love, surprisingly so right for each other. And Spencer. The man she'd married twice. The man she would marry ten times if she needed to. And of course, the baby. A little boy, she was certain. He'd be just like his daddy—strong, handsome, wonderful.

Her husband. It had taken a while, and the road had been rocky, but he'd made all her dreams come true. Every one. He reached out his hand and she took it. She leaned on him all the way down the aisle.

COMING NEXT MONTH

#729 IT TAKES A HERO Gina Wilkins
Bachelor Auction

Romance author Kristin Cole didn't need a man—she needed a hero! With writer's block staring her in the face, Kristin couldn't resist bidding on gorgeous Perry Goodman, just for inspiration. But Perry wasn't a one-night hero. He was holding out for a "happily ever after"—one that included her....

#730 LOGAN'S WAY Lisa Ann Verge

Ambushed! That's how Dr. Logan Macallistair felt when his peaceful retreat was invaded by a sexy redhead. The indomitable Eugenia Van Saun, Ph.D.—botanist with an attitude—was using his cabin for research? He'd been alone and he wanted to stay that way. Still, looking at Ginny, he had a growing appreciation for flowers, the birds and the bees...and who better to explore them with?

#731 NOT IN MY BED! Kate Hoffmann
The Wrong Bed

Carrie Reynolds had only one weakness: Devlin Riley. The sexy adventurer played the starring role in all Carrie's thoughts and fantasies. When Carrie went on vacation, she wasn't particularly surprised that Devlin showed up while she slept, stroking her, seducing her.... Then she woke up—and discovered she wasn't dreaming....

#732 FORBIDDEN Janelle Denison
Blaze

For years Detective Josh Marchiano had been in love with his partner's wife. But now, Paige was a widow—and she was in danger. Torn between guilt and desire, Josh vowed to protect her at all costs. Little did he guess that he'd have to stay by her side all day...and in her bed all night!